"How can you explain my knowing you?"

Dylan's eyes searched the depths of hers. "You tell me, Ellie. *Is* there another explanation?"

She shook her head. What he was suggesting was incredible.

"Ellie, please. Think about it for a minute. Even if you don't remember me, can you deny that I've known you before? No," he said quickly as she made a move to pull away. "I'm not asking you to remember me. I can't torture you like that. And I'm not some madman out to get you. But please believe, just for a moment, what I'm saying—we two have shared a lifetime of love. Does it seem so impossible to you?"

Did it? No denying it, he knew her. But had they loved each other? And if they had, *why had she forgotten him?*

Dear Reader,

Welcome to the fourth great month of CELEBRATION 1000! We're winding up this special event with fireworks!— six more dazzling love stories that will light up your summer nights. The festivities begin with *Impromptu Bride* by beloved author Annette Broadrick. While running for their lives, Graham Douglas and Katie Kincaid had to marry. But will their hasty wedding lead to everlasting love?

Favorite author Elizabeth August will keep you enthralled with *The Forgotten Husband.* Amnesia keeps Eloise from knowing the real reason she'd married rugged, brooding Jonah Tavish. But brief memories of sweet passion keep her searching for the truth.

This month our FABULOUS FATHER is *Daniel's Daddy*— a heartwarming story by Stella Bagwell.

Debut author Kate Thomas brings us a tale of courtship— Texas-style in—*The Texas Touch.*

There's love and laughter when a runaway heiress plays *Stand-in Mom* in Susan Meier's romantic romp. And don't miss Jodi O'Donnell's emotional story of a love all but forgotten in *A Man To Remember.*

We'd love to know if you have enjoyed CELEBRATION 1000! Please write to us at the address shown below.

Happy reading!

Anne Canadeo
Senior Editor

Please address questions and book requests to:
Silhouette Reader Service
U.S.: 3010 Walden Ave., P.O. Box 1325, Buffalo, NY 14269
Canadian: P.O. Box 609, Fort Erie, Ont. L2A 5X3

A MAN TO REMEMBER
Jodi O'Donnell

Silhouette
ROMANCE™
Published by Silhouette Books
America's Publisher of Contemporary Romance

For my hardworking critique group:
Nancy Haddock, Doniece Knowles, Yvonne Jocks, Judy Whitten and
Robin Teer (1952-1992). Till we meet again.

ACKNOWLEDGMENTS:
My gratitude goes to Patrice Hein, R.N., B.S.N., and to Robert and
Susan Montero of San Ramon, California. Many thanks also go to Dora Brown
and Pamela Johnson, and to my husband, Darrel Raynor.

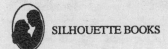 SILHOUETTE BOOKS

ISBN 0-373-19021-2

A MAN TO REMEMBER

Printed in U.S.A.

Books by Jodi O'Donnell

Silhouette Romance

Still Sweet on Him #969
The Farmer Takes a Wife #992
A Man To Remember #1021

JODI O'DONNELL

considers herself living proof that "writing what you know" works. She grew up in Iowa but moved to California—only to marry the hometown boy she'd known since fifth grade. Her first novel, *Still Sweet on Him,* won the Romance Writers of America 1992 Golden Heart Award for Best Unpublished Traditional Romance.

Jodi and her husband, Darrel, run a successful consulting business near Dallas, Texas, with the aid of their computer cat, ASCII, and wolf-hybrid pup, Rio.

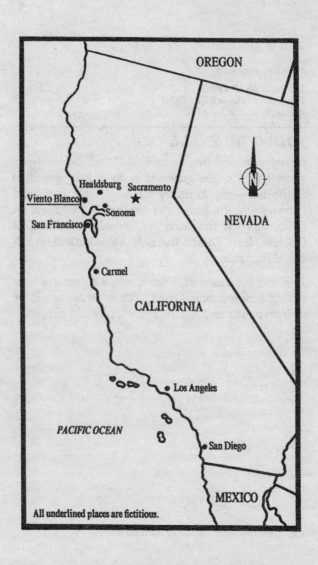

All underlined places are fictitious.

Chapter One

He came out of the mist like a giant raven on the wing.

Even within the safety of the small gallery, Elise Nash took an involuntary step backward. She'd been staring absently out the window at the gray facades of the various shops on Seaspray Avenue. The impenetrable fog that pervaded California's northern coast dulled the usually colorful buildings along the quaint street. The branches of the few trees lining the sidewalk made an indistinct pattern, like dewed spiderwebs, against the opaqueness. Tourist season had yet to arrive, and so the entire boulevard was deserted.

Until he appeared.

He split the dense, unmoving atmosphere as he glided down the street, gaining substance in his approach. Elise realized where she'd gotten the impression of preying darkness in flight: the man was all in black. Even his hair was black, a dusky ebony that absorbed the muted daylight. Though not a breeze stirred the air, the tails of his long duster coat streamed out behind him as one long-legged stride after another brought him closer.

He seemed about to pass by, continuing on some critical course, when he stopped across the road from her. He stared into the interior of the gallery, his deep-set eyes storming its sanctuary. Elise took another step backward and hoped he hadn't seen her watching him. But her move put her directly under one of the spotlights meant to showcase the painting on display.

His head reared back as a slap of recognition hit his features. He mouthed her name. *Elise.*

A shiver of foreboding scurried up her spine as she realized she was the object of his purposeful advance. Before she could react, he'd crossed the narrow road in four steps and jerked open the gallery's door.

Elise pivoted toward him. The cluster of bells, which usually tinkled cheerfully at the arrival of a customer, instead tolled a knell as the door slammed shut behind him.

His gaze devoured her in a way that spoke of desperate relief. His lips were bloodless and his chest rose and fell in evidence of the strong emotion surging through him. Tension radiated from his stance, feet spread wide and fists nailed to his sides, as if he didn't trust his impulses. Her own impulses told her to run, yet Elise remained rooted by eyes like midnight, their pupils lost in the surrounding blackness.

"Elise," he grated out. Longing ravaged his face. "My God, Ellie, I've been looking for you forever."

With that he closed the distance between them. His hands clamped over her upper arms, and he pulled her against him.

Elise gasped. Real terror rose in her throat as she realized his intent. She tried to turn her head but found his mouth already on hers, invading it. And she felt herself drowning in a powerful kiss.

It overran her senses. He'd brought with him the scent of sea tang, and it wrapped itself around her as surely as he did. His harsh intake of breath was followed by a forceful exhalation against her cheek as life-giving air rushed between them. Slick material dampened her palms as she pressed them against his chest in resistance. Her feeble attempts at freedom, however, were no match against the purpose in his embrace. His mouth drew on hers as if he could not get enough of her. He possessed her with the fervor of a man who'd come far and fought hard for this reward.

On and on it went, that soul-invading kiss. It held her spellbound, like a wild animal in the beam of a headlight, frightening and mesmerizing her at the same time. Some force in him seemed to reach out to her, into her, searching for something he'd found there before. *Impossible.* He was a stranger. And yet Elise felt a similar force rise up in her as if challenged. For an instant, she responded to this man, or tried to, straining as a hand would toward another across a chasm, struggling as a life would on the brink of destruction.

But then the chasm widened, a splitting of the very foundation on which she stood. Whatever fragile strand of connection she'd sensed snapped.

She gave a dry sob of defeat. Or denial.

He tore his lips from hers and crushed her to him. "God, I missed you, too," he whispered, evidently drawing his own conclusion about the sound she'd made. His hands came up to frame her face, his fingers digging into her hair.

"Elise. If you only knew...I thought I was crazy. I couldn't believe how you just weren't *there.*" He kissed her again, hard. *"Why?"* he asked. "Just tell me why. Why did you disappear without a word?"

Obsidian eyes bore into hers, took over the anguished searching his lips had begun, and pulled at her with their startling intimacy, as if he did indeed know her, heart and soul.

Did he? Did she know him?

Her confusion suspended for the moment as Elise lifted one shaking hand, and her fingertips grazed his cheek in tentative exploration. At her touch, his eyes drifted closed on a barely stifled groan. Relieved of that sharp scrutiny, his face lost its ferociousness, and Elise studied him, looking for some sign of prior knowledge.

He had well-defined features. Her artist's eye appraised them, the finely chiseled planes of cheek and chin and nose that hinted at exotic blood. And yet his skin lacked any swarthiness. On the contrary, his face, Elise saw, was as white as his lips, the shadow of a day-old beard rimming them and shading his jaw and throat. Blue-black hair, damp and disheveled, surrounded that face. A handsome face, she thought. A haunted face.

You just weren't there.

A stranger's face. Wasn't it?

"I don't...know," she said.

His eyes sprang open. She saw the flaring of his eyelids at the expression in her own eyes, and she realized he thought she'd responded to his question. Slowly, he shook his head in a mixture of disbelief and perplexity.

"What's wrong, Ellie?" he asked. "Has something happened?"

At his words, Elise felt a wresting within her chest as if now two forces opposed each other, battled for control. Her fingers curled reflexively, her short nails making an imprint on his sandpapered skin. *What, indeed, has happened?*

She jerked her hand away as if burned. Her alarm returned. She tried to free herself.

His grip tightened on her arms. "What's happened, Elise? Tell me!"

"Let me go!" Vaguely, Elise realized she struggled more against the conflict that had sprung up within her than with this stranger. And yet she must get away from him!

In her head began a deep, dull pounding.

Elise jumped when the front door crashed open, the string of bells jangling discordantly as they rebounded against the wooden frame. Another man stood in the doorway, his expression as forbidding as the dark stranger's had been a moment before when he'd stood in the same spot.

"Keith," Elise breathed in relief. The stranger let her go, and she leaned against the counter behind her, bracing her palms on either side of her as her blood set a punishing pace through the vessels in her brain.

"What's going on here?" Keith Hurston asked, his tone wary and suspicious. His glance shifted from her to the other man.

Elise's mouth fell open. Her spine stiffened with indignation despite her shaky reaction to the tall man in black. "Keith!"

"Who's he?" the stranger asked her, his voice filled with the same suspicion.

Her unbelieving gaze switched to him. "I might ask the same of you!"

He looked as if she'd struck him. *"What?"*

Keith placed himself between them. "Do you know this man, Elise?"

She hesitated, a bid to grasp more firmly the wisp of a perception drifting just out of reach. The brief connection she'd experienced with this stranger had disappeared. Yet why had she felt it at all?

Because you want answers, too. Answers you haven't been able to find within yourself.

A sharp pulse of pain constricted over one entire side of her skull. Elise gasped and grabbed the edge of the counter for balance.

Keith stepped to her side. "Elise! Are you all right?"

She pressed the heel of her hand to her temple and nodded impatiently, feeling powerless against her body's weakness. "It's one of those spasms."

From the corner of her eye, she saw the stranger move toward her in sudden concern. "What is it? What's wrong with her?"

Keith rounded on the other man. "It's none of your business!"

The stranger's eyes narrowed. "And just what business is it of yours?"

Keith slid his arm around her shoulders, and Elise slumped against him as another wave of pain hit her. "I'm the man she's going to marry," he said, oddly defiant.

Again, the stranger looked as if he'd been struck. He emitted a low growl of disbelief as he took another step forward. Keith let go of her and assumed an equally aggressive stance. Elise realized the two men would come to blows if no one intervened.

"Stop it, both of you!" she cried. Though her head pounded furiously, she shoved away from the counter and laid a warning hand on each man's arm. "I don't know what's going on here, but fighting isn't going to solve anything!"

Neither Keith nor the stranger moved, though their gazes remained locked, their bodies taut and ready should the other twitch a muscle.

"Tell him, Elise," the stranger said with grim satisfaction in his black eyes. "Tell him who I am."

"But I don't know who you are!"

His gaze whipped to hers. Shocked betrayal assaulted her, shot from his eyes straight into her heart. "Dammit, what *is* going on here? It's *me,* Elise—Dylan. Are you saying you don't know me?"

She could only stare at him, unable to respond to his appeal. *Dylan.* The name meant nothing to her.

Under eclipsing black brows, a dark storm built in his eyes, as if he already knew she'd not support his contention that they shared some sort of acquaintance. But the fact was she didn't know this man.

He spoke with such sureness, though, with such conviction. Was it possible?

With effort, Elise racked her already tortured brain. Instead of an answer, that sense of unholy conflict assailed her. A realization clambered to the front of her mind, calling for her attention: No, she didn't know him, but there was a powerful threat here.

Yet this time, instead of making her want to flee in fright, anger boiled up in her, urging her to confront the threat head-on. *You've no right to treat me this way. No one has.*

Strangely, the throbbing in her head subsided.

Elise walked calmly to the door and opened it. "Please leave," she said without a trace of a quiver in her voice.

"No," the stranger argued. "I don't know what's happened, but I won't go until I find out."

"Find out what?"

"How it is you don't know me. It's . . . impossible. What about my letters—"

"Leave!" This time her voice shook with every bit of her anger. She had to get this man out of here before tenuous control splintered and the pain engulfed her again.

He took a step forward, hand extended in entreaty. "Elise—"

Keith's fingers caught the stranger's wrist. "You heard her, pal."

The other man ignored the threat in Keith's voice, his scrutiny hard upon Elise. She met his probing inquiry and found nothing in that gaze she recognized. She did see there, however, a confusion as earthshaking as hers had been a few minutes earlier. And she saw a very real concern for her that softened her own gaze.

"I'm fine," she said quietly, answering at least one of the questions she read in his eyes. "Now, please . . . go."

Obviously reluctant, he nodded. With a quick upward twist of his forearm, he broke Keith's hold in a manner that implied trained defense skills. He threw a last challenging look at her fiancé, and one at her that fairly shouted *I'll be back*. Then dark stranger whirled and was gone.

Elise turned to Keith as his arms surrounded her. She rested her forehead against his shoulder. A wave of lightheadedness swamped her as her heartbeat slowed to normal. That's likely what had made her head hurt so badly, she thought. She wasn't used to such strong emotions rocketing through her. Yet when she'd been angry, the pain had vanished. At least it had in this instance. The discovery puzzled her. She'd made a point of avoiding stress since her accident, tried to keep herself on an even keel while she got her life back on course. And it had been weeks since she'd gotten one of those spasms.

Within her, discouragement sparked and flared momentarily before she found the strength to douse it with resolve: *I am getting better.*

"So who was that guy?" Keith asked, distracting her from her reflections.

"I told you, I don't know." Elise raised her head and found him watching her, judging her—and not believing her. She pulled out of his grasp, remembering the way he'd looked at her, wary, with the same accusation in his eyes. "Do you think I'm lying?"

"Do you think it unreasonable for me to wonder exactly what's going on when I find the woman I'm going to marry in another man's arms?"

Elise lowered her lashes. He had a point. "I wasn't there willingly. Surely you saw that."

"Yes," he said slowly, "but you did hesitate when he asked if you knew him."

"It was an instinctive reaction! He was so utterly certain, for just an instant I questioned myself." Elise cupped her elbows in icy palms. She wouldn't let doubt intrude again, bringing that crippling pain with it.

Yet she turned away from Keith, doubt worming its way past her defenses anyway. Or was it guilt? She wasn't lying to Keith, but neither was she telling the complete truth, for she had felt *something* with that man, however brief. Recognition? Or perhaps a premonition? Not of things past, but of things to come.

Elise ran her hand through her hair as a disturbing thought struck her. "My God, how did he know my name?"

She felt Keith's hands hover above her shoulders in hesitation, then settle there. "Your aunt mentioned he asked for you," he said, the statement brief but portending.

"He went to Aunt Charlotte's?" Elise turned to face him. "He knows where I live?" A sense of true violation temporarily overtook rational thought. "Is Aunt Char all right?"

"I was able to reassure her. Seems a man had come by the house wanting to know where you were," he said, his eyes shuttered but observant. "She thought he might be...an old friend from Oregon or something. She said she realized after she'd told him where you worked that she might have made a mistake giving out information about you. So she called me, and I came over here. I'm glad I was in town today. I could have just as easily not been."

"Why didn't Aunt Char call me, ask me?" Elise asked. But she knew the answer to that question. Nearly four months had passed since the automobile accident that had forced Elise into her elderly aunt's care. She'd almost completely recovered, yet in both Keith's and Charlotte's eyes she was still unwell and needed to be protected from any upset. Likely Aunt Char, who herself never dealt well with upset in her life, had phoned the first person whom she thought capable of handling any questionable situation. Once Keith had been alerted, she'd probably set her mind at rest and not even realized Elise could use a bit of notice, too. Or that Elise could have handled the problem herself.

Elise sighed. Why was it so difficult to remember Aunt Charlotte was a seventy-six-year-old woman who'd never been particularly self-reliant? *You shouldn't expect so much of people,* she scolded herself.

She peered up at Keith. "So why didn't *you* call and warn me before coming over?"

"Good thing I didn't. It seems I got here just in time. Who knows what kind of nut he was, or what he meant to do to you. I'm taking you home, and then I'm calling the sheriff."

Elise frowned, feeling she still hadn't gotten an answer. "You're overreacting a little, don't you think?"

"Am I?"

She thought a moment, clearly picturing the tall man who'd looked at her with such yearning and need. And concern. She didn't think he meant to harm her. Despite his actions, the threat she'd felt hadn't been physical. On the other hand, the way he'd held her and kissed her had certainly been obsessive. Almost fanatical.

"Elise," Keith said when she remained silent, "Viento Blanco is a small, very safe town, but it's still a tourist town. No one here looks twice at a stranger. What's to stop a person with God knows what on his mind from coming into town and asking some discreet questions about a young woman he saw at one of the shops? With that information, he could look up an address in the phone book. Charlotte is the only Nash listed. And then he'd go to her house, claiming he knows you."

"But why would he ask her where I was, if he'd been watching me? He'd already know where I worked."

Keith lowered his brows disapprovingly.

"I'm not defending him," she explained, a little exasperated. "I'm just trying to make some sense out of this whole situation." *And I still don't know what the stranger wanted.*

"I think you're being naive, Elise."

She dropped her chin and inspected the weave of her cotton ramie sweater. Although Keith wasn't stating it outright, he suspected what the stranger wanted from her. The afternoon might have gone quite differently, she realized, had she been a bit more trusting, a bit more gullible. She'd almost been taken in by this man's particular version of *Haven't we met somewhere before?* The scary part was, she *wasn't* a trusting person—and yet such conviction had been hard to refute, hard to resist. But as she'd admitted to Keith, in the face of the stranger's certitude, any rational being would have at least hesitated. Wouldn't they? Or, in her weakened state of health, was she particularly susceptible to the power of suggestion?

Trepidation stole over her as she thought of how she'd responded to the stranger. For the flash of an instant, she'd wanted to believe him.

Because you want answers. Answers you haven't been able to find within yourself.

What if the stranger came back? After the way he'd acted, was there any doubt that he wouldn't? When he did, what would she do? What could he do to her? Maybe she should do as Keith advised and let him take her home.

"No," she said rebelliously and caught the look of censure in Keith's eye. "I won't live in fear in this small town, at the place I work, in my own home." Here, it seemed, was the solidifying of that premonition she'd sensed earlier: If she allowed fear to be the driving force in her life, she'd never recover completely from the accident that had torn her world from its moorings and set her adrift without her most beloved occupation.

"He practically attacked you, Elise," Keith protested.

"I can't be afraid to go about my life!" she cut in. Then, realizing she had nothing to gain by acting agitated, she said more calmly, "I'm not saying there's no need for caution, but really I don't think the man meant me physical harm."

"How do you know?"

"I . . . know." As an artist, who tuned herself in to emotions as a part of the creative process, she knew a gut feeling when it hit. "If he'd truly wanted to spirit me away for evil purposes, he would hardly have been conspicuously aggressive, storming into the gallery like that. I know it."

"How very reassuring for me."

Elise regarded Keith with exasperated affection. From behind wire-rimmed glasses, his gray eyes stoutheartedly returned her tenderness. Here, too, was very real concern for her.

He was a big man, husky and solid, like a great bear. Over the past four months, he'd been the anchor that had kept her from sinking into the shifting sands of constant change her life had become.

Keith Hurston had managed Aunt Charlotte's affairs for years, and so he'd been the one she'd turned to when she found herself once again faced with caring for her grandniece, this time a severely injured one. Elise had known Keith as a teenager, when she'd come to live with her aunt after Elise's parents died, themselves victims of a violent auto accident. On her return to Viento Blanco, Keith had taken over the matters she'd been too ill—and Aunt Charlotte, too fragile—to handle. He'd been there when the two women had consulted with doctors, offering advice and helping them make decisions on treatment and therapy. When Elise had felt strong enough to begin the journey back to a normal existence, he'd given her a job at one of the investment properties he owned. Though it required little more than waiting on a trickle of clientele, managing Hurston Gallery was the perfect interim position for her, one meant to ease her back into her real work as an artist.

The support Keith had provided, the patience he still showed in dealing with her not always rational aunt had touched Elise deeply. He'd been as patient and steadfast when she'd known him years ago—too much so, she realized now, for a girl who could have used a stronger presence in her life to break through her isolation and help her recover from her parents' deaths. But no such personality had ever come to her rescue. No one had realized she'd needed help. In a way, no one had cared.

Now, though, Keith's constancy and her need for such security in her life seemed to mesh. When he'd asked her to marry him, she'd said yes. The plan was that after the wedding Keith would find someone else to run the gallery. Then Elise could concentrate on accumulating inventory for her own show, one that he would set up and sponsor, taking care of every detail for her. All she had to do was paint.

In a mere five days' time, she realized, she and Keith Hurston would be married.

Desolation, like an icy wind off the ocean, permeated her bones. What would happen then? In less than a week she would have no reason to put off that moment when she faced a blank canvas again. Irrationally, she wondered for an instant if they should postpone the small ceremony with the justice of the peace.

And what reason would she give Keith for such a delay? Hadn't she just told him she wouldn't let fear dictate her actions? She needed to push on, in fact. She was at a plateau in her recovery, that was all; a comfortable resting place. Her doctor had told her she would reach this stage and that she would naturally feel apprehensive about moving forward. And though getting back into the studio might be just what she needed, today had shown her she still had a long way to go to complete recovery—meaning she didn't need any more upsets like the one this stranger had created.

"All right," she agreed. "Alert the sheriff to this man's presence in town. Maybe they can give him a warning or something."

Keith nodded. "I'll stop by the station after I take you home."

She glanced at the clock. "But it's only three-thirty."

"And not a soul in sight." He brushed the back of his fingers across her cheek and gave her a mock stern father-knows-best look. "I'm not going to lose hundreds of dollars in revenue over the next few hours. You have my permission to take the rest of the day off."

Elise opened her mouth to protest yet again. She thought she'd made it clear she didn't want to let this episode disrupt their lives. But she knew she should check on Aunt Charlotte. Even with Keith's assurances that her aunt seemed fine, Elise wanted to confirm this for herself.

"It's only a quarter mile in broad daylight," she pointed out.

"Elise, that guy's still out there," Keith countered.

"Maybe he is. Or maybe he'll have left town by now, seeing as how I didn't fall for his story. In any case, I can't go around constantly looking over my shoulder or wondering who's around the next corner." She gazed at him in appeal. "I won't live like that, Keith." *I'd never recover then.*

"I understand, darling. Do it for me, then, the old Hurston fusspot."

That made her smile. He really was dear to worry about her so. She nodded her agreement and he tugged her close for a quick kiss. "Good. I'll go by the police station right after I drop you off. And I'll be over tonight, no argument."

Elise slid into her raincoat, tucking her mist-plagued mane, a constant condition in this climate, under her collar. She stepped outside to wait on the stoop for him, her gaze involuntarily sweeping the area, while Keith pulled the shutters closed, locked them and finished closing up.

With the thick fog keeping visibility to a hundred feet or so, she saw little, out of the ordinary or not. Many of the shops were still closed for the winter and wouldn't open for another month. Other shopkeepers remained open year-round, needing even the scant off-season income. Or they had no other business to occupy their time. Like her.

Elise wrapped her arms around her middle. No, she hadn't picked up brush or charcoal since her accident. She'd simply found nothing that compelled her to do so. Once more, desolation filled her chest. Once more, she pushed it down. It was simply incomprehensible that she would never again know that feeling of filling a canvas with vibrant images conjured, as if by magic, from the depths her heart, mind and soul.

What stopped her, though? Did she fear what she might call forth, should she try to rouse her muse? Perhaps it would be a being she hardly recognized, who'd changed and evolved in the months left to itself.

Keith pulled the door shut behind him and put his arm around her, giving her shoulder a squeeze. "Ready, darling?"

Elise nodded, and they started up the street in silence.

She knew what really terrified her, and it wasn't a tall, dark stranger. No, what Elise feared most in this world was that she'd face that snowy linen canvas—and find nothing. Nothing at all.

Dylan Colman sank into the shadows between two buildings and watched the couple hurry past. His eyes fixed upon her form alone, following it until it was out of sight. Then he leaned his head back against the rough brick wall and swallowed past the mass of pain lodged in his throat.

He'd found her. And she didn't know him. He pounded the butt of one fist against the wall. What torment it had been to feel her search his face with her talented hands and find no recognition, when he'd ached countless times for one trace of her skill to depict from memory that wild hair, its color the same rich, melting toffee brown as her eyes. He'd have paid a king's ransom for the ability to render each fine curve and line of the beloved features that had been indelibly sketched upon the inside of his eyelids night after sleepless night.

But never had he pictured her with that look of mystification. That look that told him he was a total stranger to her.

It still didn't seem real. He was ready to question his own sanity rather than believe it. The only thing he felt certain of was that she hadn't been faking her reaction to him.

He pushed away from the wall, driving his hands into his coat pockets as he paced the damp, narrow space. During the time he'd looked for her, of all the possibilities of why she'd left that he'd pondered, agonized over, never had he imagined this, that she simply wouldn't know him. Or that she'd fear him.

It was inconceivable. *They loved each other.* They were going to be married. He wanted to tell her that, wanted to shake it into her, wanted to show her in the wonderfully diverse ways he'd dreamed of showing her during their separation.

But she didn't know him. And she was engaged to another man.

She *had* known him, though! For one brief instant, recognition had flickered in her eyes. Yet it had made her afraid.

Dylan swore soundly. *Calm down,* he thought, inhaling deeply. He had to abandon that line of thinking for now, or he'd drive himself crazy. The question was *why* didn't she know him? How was it possible that she wouldn't? Leaning against the wall once again, he searched his memory for a clue, went over every conversation they'd had together, his thoughts following a well-known, well-traveled path.

He'd known hers was a special soul the first time he'd seen her. Her artist's eye and temperament made her as sensitive as litmus paper to her environment. Like a sponge, she absorbed far more than the average person—but she poured it all out again, and more, through her work. Through her love.

She wasn't an easy person to get to know, and he had felt an elevation of his own existence when he'd been able to draw her out. He'd never felt anything like it, being the object of that focus, being the recipient of its expression. It had brought him across thousands of miles to find her. And now that he had, he wouldn't lose her again.

With a start, Dylan realized he'd been standing in the same position for an hour. The dampness had crept into his very marrow. At least it was a change, after days and days of the constant sun and dryness in which he'd been living. It was a whole different country—no, a whole different world from this place—and he had to go back there in barely a week. This time, he wouldn't go without Elise. Not again. That had been his mistake before: duty had called, and where it drew him could be frightening for the uninitiated. The hesitant. And what he'd resisted facing was that she had had doubts about the two of them, even at the peak of their immersion in one another, and that's why she'd stayed behind.

He understood, of course. Things had happened so quickly between them. He'd believed that the time apart would be good for them, that the love between them was strong enough to survive the separation. He had thought it better to wait for the two of them to be together.

He'd been wrong.

Dylan glanced up. Dusk was settling, though the change from dull, overcast daylight to an equally dull twilight was barely discernible. He couldn't stay here all night, waiting for the morning and another glimpse of a woman whose golden eyes filled with fear at the sight of him. Again, frustration strained in him like a dog against its chain. It just wasn't possible to forget someone you love!

Unless she didn't love him anymore. Or never really had.

It was a fear that had plagued him throughout his search for her. She'd covered her tracks so well, as if she hadn't wanted anyone to follow her. When he finally did find her, he'd been determined to ask her if that were her intent. He wanted to see her face when she told him yes, she meant to desert him and their love. He never dreamed she would do it so thoroughly.

Dylan sighed roughly. He could use a hot meal and shower. And rest. Maybe tomorrow he'd be thinking more clearly. So far, nothing had produced even the slightest clue as to what was going on. He rubbed the back of his head tiredly, weary from the effort of trying to piece together an impossibly awry puzzle.

His chin jerked upward. *Her head.* She'd held her head in pain. Spasms, she'd said. So she was ill—or had been recently. And perhaps somehow she'd lost what she knew of him, lost that brief moment when they had known each other's hearts and souls and bodies with a certainty that no amount of time or distance or change could erase. But it had.

Was it possible, then, that she *had* forgotten him? How? And again the question assailed him: *Why?*

Chapter Two

Elise glanced out the window just as a streetlight came on. The fog cordoned off its candlepower, allowing only a concentrated circle of illumination around the light's globe into the enveloping gloom. Although the Viento Blanco peninsula and surrounding bay, with their rugged, picturesque coastline and sparkling white sand beaches, were considered jewels in the northern coast, half the year the area suffered under the yoke of a depressing and omnipresent fog that discouraged a permanent infiltration of people. Elise had hated that fog as a teenager, living with her aunt, and she hated it even more now. The weather seemed to sap her strength, to close around her like a prison cell. Her still healing bones ached.

God, she missed her home in Oregon! The state had its share of rainfall and overcast days, to be sure, but the fog was curbed by the mountains, lush with evergreens so intensely verdant the color reverberated against the sky. And the sky... When the mists cleared, the sky was such an acute shade of blue it was forever burned into the retina of her eye. From the deck of her rustic studio, she'd spent many hours contemplating that view, drawing inspiration.

It wasn't her studio any longer, she realized. Keith had traveled to Oregon a few months ago to settle her affairs there, since she couldn't go herself. He said the landlord had rented the cabin to someone else when two months had gone by without a sign of her. The owner had been sorry to hear about her trouble, sorry he'd had to sell some of her things to pay for moving and storing what remained, but he'd been quick to point out to Keith that he'd had no idea what had happened to her. For weeks, in fact, her landlord hadn't even known she was gone. By the time he'd discovered her disappearance and filed a missing-person report, Keith told Elise, any trail she'd left as to her whereabouts was obscured by the time that had elapsed and the bizarre circumstances of her accident. In fact, because her rental car had burned to a cinder, and the means to identify her with it, no one had known who she was as she'd lain in a coma for days. And when she'd finally become cognizant enough to tell them her name, to have them notify Charlotte Nash in Viento Blanco, no one had thought of notifying her landlord in Oregon—not Aunt Charlotte or Keith, certainly not herself. She'd been too busy fighting for her life.

Yes, Elise understood that her landlord had done what he'd thought best, even though she once would have guessed he'd have done more for her. But their relationship, while friendly, had been essentially distant; she was wrong to expect more from him. And she was sorry, too. The news that she no longer had a real home had disturbed her as nothing else had since her accident. The cabin had been her retreat; she'd been saving to buy it.

And she would some day, she vowed. When she was well again.

Now, though, she sat in a darkened living room, having been banished there by Charlotte. Through the arched doorway came the diffused light from the kitchen, connected to the living room by the dining room. Elise heard her aunt puttering, preparing dinner. She'd have preferred the reverse, with Charlotte relaxing while she fixed the meal, but her aunt had insisted she rest after her "terrible scare" today. Elise was afraid that would happen. Aunt Char's mouth had been a round *O* of distress earlier, as she'd watched Elise ascend the front steps on Keith's arm. He had promptly told Charlotte about the episode at the gallery. He'd known Elise would keep the details to herself, he said, and quite rightly she would have, since her aunt hardly needed that kind of agitation. But Keith had felt Elise would downplay any effect the event might have on her and overexert herself.

As if I'm more infirm than my seventy-six-year-old aunt, Elise thought with irritation. She had an overwhelming urge to vent her frustration like a rebellious child—a child who knew she had no say about her own life and therefore sought control in any way possible.

What did one do when defying authority? Elise wondered. Hold her breath till she turned blue? Refuse to eat? Run away from home?

She contemplated the drab scene outside the window. The last option held little appeal. And lest she forget, a stranger lurked out there in the mist. No, it wasn't her own fear that held her captive, she thought ruefully. It was a big bad wolf of a man with evil on his mind.

Abruptly, Elise rose and switched on a lamp, glancing around for something to read or do. It would be a while until dinner, hours until Keith arrived. Had she been at the gallery, she'd be doing the month-end bookkeeping. Keith had only recently, and at her insistence, turned that part of the business over to her, reminding her that his own bookkeeper was perfectly capable of continuing with the responsibility. Elise assured him repeatedly that it was no bother. In fact, she rather enjoyed the task. Accounting was so straightforward, had such a symmetry: the numbers either added up or they didn't. She took absurd satisfaction in bringing the accounts to heel.

Yet she knew the real reason she insisted on doing the books. It was because she'd go mad without something, anything, to make it seem as if she moved forward. Something that gave her a sense of purpose. To keep her from being too alone with her own thoughts. Of course, as tourist season approached, business would pick up and there'd be more to keep her occupied. Except by then she'd be married to Keith and busy with her painting.

Ironically, had she the inclination to paint, she would have savored the hours of solitude that working in the gallery provided. In her studio in Oregon, she'd gone days, weeks, without seeing another person. She hadn't needed normal discourse. When she immersed herself in her art, she went to different places, resided on an entirely separate plane of reality, apart and alone, but in a wholly satisfying way.

With a start, she realized she hadn't even thought of Keith a few moments before as she'd sat there dreaming of going back to Oregon.

Suddenly restless, Elise walked through the dining room and stopped just outside the kitchen door. Aunt Charlotte, her back to Elise, was busy stirring something that made her ample backside, covered in violet gray wool, quiver like an aspen in the breeze. A very full aspen.

"Aunt Char," she said softly, breaking the silence as gently as possible.

The older woman jumped anyway and glanced over her shoulder, the lenses of her glasses briefly reflecting the overhead light and giving her a curiously blank-eyed appearance.

She smiled at her niece. "Getting hungry?" she asked.

Elise found herself nodding, though food was the furthest thing from her mind right now. "How long till dinner?"

"I've almost got these biscuits mixed up and...oh, heavens, I forgot to add the egg noodles to the chicken soup." She reached for the plastic bag on the counter before realizing her hands were covered with flour and dough.

Elise stepped to her side. "Let me." She opened the package and dumped the noodles into the stock already filled with pieces of chicken and vegetables. "Mmm. Smells delicious. Need any help?"

Aunt Charlotte shook her head in a way that told Elise she had too many things to think of at once. Her aunt was easily flustered—and much too old to shoulder the burden of being a full-time caretaker. Charlotte was the one who deserved to be cared for.

Before Elise's parents died, her father had always looked after his maiden aunt, his father's only sister, advising her in business and seeing to her affairs from Elise's family home near Boston. Charlotte had depended on him completely and had been as devastated as Elise by his death. Even then, Charlotte had been ill equipped to handle the grieving, introverted teenager who had become her only living relative. And seven years later, Elise knew Charlotte had even less ability to tend to a convalescing adult.

"Can I do anything else to help?" Elise repeated patiently.

"No, dear," Aunt Charlotte answered. She floured the rim of a glass and pressed it into the rolled-out dough. "I just need to get these biscuits into a hot oven."

Elise glanced down and covertly turned the oven dial from OFF to 425°. "So how long until we eat?" she asked once more, again with gentle patience.

"What? Oh, I'd say a half hour or so."

"That leaves me just enough time," Elise said, slipping past her aunt to the back porch. Her still damp raincoat hung on a peg, and she gave it a shake before putting it on. "I want to run down to the gallery and pick up some work."

Aunt Charlotte spun around in a cloud of flour. "But what about that man?" she asked, pale blue eyes wide behind her glasses. "Keith said he might come back."

"The police are on the lookout for him," Elise said calmly, though annoyance rose in her as she silently berated Keith for spooking her aunt. "And I'm not being naive when I say that I really believe he wasn't out to hurt me."

Quite the contrary, she thought. In her mind's eye, she saw coal black eyes awash with pain, as if *she* had hurt *him*.

She wound a scarf around her head. "They've probably seen him by now and warned him. And besides, I'll have to walk back and forth from the gallery tomorrow, and the next day after that and the next," she said, emphasizing the ongoing situation.

"But it isn't safe!" Charlotte cried.

"It's perfectly safe," Elise said firmly. "The street is well lit, and other shop owners will be closing up and walking home at this hour." She had spent so long trussed up in a hospital bed, she'd become vigilant about protecting her autonomy. And after that lapse in her strength today, she was almost desperate to get out on her own, however small the effort. She simply couldn't be a prisoner again.

Elise bent forward and rubbed a smudge of flour from Charlotte's cheek, replacing it with a kiss. "I'll be back in a flash."

Five minutes later, Elise had reached the gallery and gathered the papers she needed. She stuffed the ledgers into a brown paper bag with sturdy plastic handles—a small precaution that would keep her hands free, though she truly believed she had nothing to fear. Locking the door behind her, she was reassured by the friendly greeting called by the owner of the blown-glass shop across the street. Elise waved and watched him walk away in the opposite direction. She hooked the handles of the bag over her forearm and started home.

She hadn't gone twenty feet when she felt the strangest sensation of a wave of heat sweeping over her, like the fiery blast from an oven. Every hair on her body crackled with a charge of static electricity. The dampness that lived in her bones disappeared, and she broke into an instantaneous sweat.

Someone was here.

Aunt Charlotte had been right, Elise thought. She shouldn't have left the house, not with night falling. She abhorred cowardice but knew it for a logical reaction to danger, as opposed to foolhardiness. And she should have known better. So what she'd do is return to the gallery, lock the door behind her, and telephone Keith to pick her up.

Relieved to have a plan, Elise turned and took a purposeful step back toward the gallery.

A silhouette separated from the shadows and placed itself in her path.

Elise tried to scream, but no sound made it past the terror that gagged her. A large hand reached out and took her arm, pulling her into the dark crevice between two buildings.

She found her voice. "No!" she screamed, struggling against the iron grip with little effect. *Go for the eyes, the crotch.* The instruction came to her from somewhere, and she lunged for his face. He was too quick for her, though, catching her wrists in an even more restricting hold. Her brown bag caught on his elbow and tore like tissue, spilling papers and notebooks onto the pavement.

Panting, she tried the other alternative, bringing her knee up, but her leg was hampered by her long coat. He guessed her intent anyway, and Elise found herself facing a brick wall, its clammy, gritty surface abrading her cheek as the stranger's long, hard body pressed against her back, holding her immobile. Powerless. Her throat convulsed in purely instinctive panic.

Oh, God, she thought on a small gasp, trying to catch her breath. *Please don't let this happen.* Had she fought so hard, made it this far back, only to die at the hands of a maniac?

She'd been so sure he meant her no harm. Her instincts had told her so.

The very instincts that had been barren of fruit for months now.

"Elise." His voice, close to her ear, was ragged with its own pain. "I'm not going to hurt you. I promise I'd never hurt you."

She made a sound of disbelief.

"For God's sake," he said roughly, "believe that one thing even if you can't believe anything else. Please, Ellie."

She felt the pressure on her back decrease slightly, as if he would release her should she accept his statement. Elise nodded jerkily.

His hold eased and he turned her with gentle hands that almost made her believe him. She shied reflexively when he raised his hand to her face, but he merely brushed back the strands of hair glued to her cheek by the damp wall. His touch was warm.

By now, night had fallen. The old-fashioned streetlamps Elise had spoken of so reassuringly to Charlotte did indeed cast a comforting glow, their light reaching even this hiding place between the buildings, though not strongly enough to reveal all of its secrets.

She stared up at the stranger, his black eyes stark in a white face that betrayed a fear of his own. What was *he* afraid of? she wondered.

"The police know about you," Elise said with false bravado, playing on that fear in case it would make a difference. "This is a small town, and you've been identified as someone who's not welcome here. So if you're thinking of..." She swallowed. "I mean if I—"

"You mean if you turn up missing or dead in some culvert, they'll know who did it and I'll live my life as a fugitive of the law?" he ruthlessly sketched the image she'd been unable to.

She flinched at the tone of his voice, and her reaction seemed to anger him.

"Isn't that what you were thinking?" Suppressed fury rimmed his mouth. "But I came out of nowhere, didn't I, Elise? I'm a total stranger to you, without a past. I could disappear back into oblivion just as easily, and no one would miss me."

He was trying to scare her as surely as she tried to scare him, damn him.

"I'm not afraid of you," she said. Completely unnerved, yes, but she wouldn't be afraid.

To her surprise, a corner of his mouth lifted. Was it her imagination or did she see a glint of relief in his eye?

"Good," he said. "Maybe you'll be able to tell me a few things, then."

Almost casually, he dug his hands into his coat pockets, the rigidity in his stance relaxing, but just barely. He wanted to talk. Fine, she thought. It bought her time. And if she could get him to let down his guard even further, she might be able to get past him.

Elise sent a stealthy glance toward the opening to the street, gauging the distance to freedom. He sensed her intent, though, and placed himself between her and her escape. The move cast his face into shadow. She strained to see his expression, but she might as well have been gazing into a void.

"What do you want to know?" she asked.

He hesitated, as if wondering where to begin. "Have you been ill, Elise?" he finally asked.

Of all the questions she'd expected, this one wasn't among them. She recalled the scene at the gallery today, how her head had pounded—as it was beginning to now. "You know I have," she said warily.

"No, I don't know. I can see that you're thinner, paler."

Thinner and paler than when? The question begged to be asked. Would he persist with the ridiculous premise that they knew each other?

"You said something today about spasms," he said leadingly.

"I was in a car accident." She could think of no reason to withhold that information.

"A bad one?"

"It could have been . . . fatal." She glanced in the other direction. Another brick wall, gleaming dully, sealed any outlet by that route. "I was driving down the coast road and hit a wet spot going downhill on a curve. The car went out of control, struck the embankment and flipped over. I was lucky, they said. If I'd spun the other way, I would have crashed through the guardrail and gone over the cliff."

They said. They also said she'd been found thirty feet from the fiery wreckage. She'd apparently had the presence of mind to release her seat belt and crawl out of the car. Had she remained within it, she would have gone up in flames as well.

But Elise still remembered only bits and pieces of that night or the days following it. Or even the days leading up to it. Her doctor had told her it might be years, if ever, before she remembered. The body had great powers of healing, protecting itself. When death passed so closely by, the mind created its own distance. And the threatened feeling Elise got from relating even the briefest details of her accident told her she should be glad for that distance.

"What about your injuries?" the stranger asked in a flat tone.

She glanced up. She didn't need to see his expression to be able to discern the determined control he held over himself. As if he were as devastated as she by the thought that she'd nearly lost her life. As if it took every ounce of strength he possessed not to reach out to her in comfort right now.

"I broke my collarbone, an arm and a leg. I sustained a cracked vertebra in my neck and was in a coma for three days because of a concussion."

"A concussion?"

"Yes. A pretty bad one." *A pretty scary one.* She pressed her fingertips to her temple at a sudden constriction there.

This time he couldn't restrain his actions. The stranger stepped toward her, and tender as a lover, he covered her small, cold hand as it lay against her cheek with his large, warm one. There was no mistaking the anguish in his eyes.

Elise froze, momentarily paralyzed by the familiarity of both his gesture and that look.

"Does it always hurt here?" he asked.

"N-no," she stammered, nearly overwhelmed by the compassion that seemed to flow like an electric current from his hand, through hers, and into her pulsing brain. "The pain migrates from front to back, but always on the right side of my head."

"And it hurts, now," he said. A statement.

"Yes," she answered, because she wanted him to know that he'd caused her pain, although it seemed he already knew. "The headaches were quite intense directly following my accident, then they tapered off. I hadn't had one in weeks—until today."

He massaged the area she'd described with a touch that tingled.

"Even though you've probably been to hell and back in the last few months, all I can think of right now is thank God you're alive," he breathed. He had turned so that the light revealed his face. "You do know, Ellie, if I'd known you were hurt, I'd have come to you, no matter the distance or circumstances. You *know* that."

"I—" She blinked. No, she didn't know that. She didn't know him, even though there was nothing but loving concern for her in his eyes. His black stranger's eyes.

Slowly, Elise pulled away from contact with him. The movement, though controlled, still produced another wave of pain. She set her teeth against it.

"My turn," she said. "Who are you and what do you want from me?"

His hand returned to his pocket, and he studied her thoughtfully. "As I told you, my name is Dylan. Dylan Colman," he said, watching her reaction, looking, she knew, for a spark of recognition.

The name still produced not a glimmer. She let the fact show plainly on her face. "And what do you want?"

Again, a hesitation. An expectation. "I want," Dylan Colman said quietly, "for you to remember."

So he was sticking to his story. "Remember? Remember what?" she demanded.

"Us. What we were—*are* to each other."

Elise spun away from the resolute look on his face that made her almost pity him. The move brought a stab of pain so great she gasped and clutched her temple. From behind her, she heard him take a step, heard his murmur of alarm. Elise made herself straighten and draw air into her lungs. Her nose confronted a dank smell farther into the gloom.

She turned back to him, determined to fight the overwhelming pain. Determined to fight him. "There is nothing to remember. I don't know you."

"Yes, you do!" He clenched his jaw. "Elise, somewhere, locked in your mind or your heart, is your memory of me." He made the statement with dead certainty.

"I've never seen you before today," she said, just as deadly certain.

"Then how is it that I know you, Elise?"

"You know nothing!" she cried in exasperation. "You know my name, where I work, where I live." Through a haze of pain, she spared a thought for Aunt Charlotte. She'd be wondering where her niece was. Elise shot another furtive glance toward the opening behind him.

Dylan moved closer, until mere inches separated them. He was half a foot taller than her, and it hurt her neck and head even more to maintain eye contact, but look him in the eye she did. She would not shrink from him.

"I know that you're an artist," he said.

"You could have found that out from anyone."

"I know that you're a loner," he went on as if she hadn't spoken. "Independent to a fault. You hate confinement." He watched her carefully. "Though I'm not sure what's made you so reclusive, I do know that if you could, you'd spend your days in a cabin on a mountainside, away from civilization."

All true, she thought with a niggling of doubt. But none of it was substantial! He'd told her nothing a fortune-teller in a circus couldn't have told her. This was just another tactic, his rendition of *You have a deep, dark secret.*

With *and you'll meet a tall, dark stranger* as a refrain.

"You're guessing," she challenged.

"Am I? You love to sail. I taught you, took you out your first time. We took midnight walks on the beach. We did—" his eyes squeezed shut and he swallowed hard, as if his own head pulsated in pain "—we did everything together," he whispered. "But that isn't what you want to know, is it?"

He opened his eyes and raised one hand. His palm cupped her jaw, a brief pressure, then slid down and back, until his fingers caressed her nape. "I know that you have a mole right here, and your mother had one just like it."

One fingertip brushed across the raised bump of tissue, its center without nerve endings. Still, the sensation was one that made Elise feel as if he'd touched her much more intimately.

"You saw it before. This afternoon," she whispered in weak denial.

"Yes, I've seen it before, but not today. I've seen it, touched it, kissed it." He bent nearer. "Most of all, Elise, I know that when you give your love, you give it completely and eternally. More than that, you demand to be loved the same way. And this is what I am to you."

He held her captivated by his gaze, suspended in time. Impossibly, he'd brought an imaginary past together with an uncertain future to meld into a moment that was this unconditional present—where anything was possible.

Again, an awful fear rose up in her, a fear that her life was not her own. Because now, if she were to believe this stranger, neither was her past.

Her arms lifted to push him away. "You're mad!"

He tightened his hold on her. "I'm not mad!"

His proximity acted like a vacuum, a suction that seemed to draw away the carefully constructed protection she'd surrounded herself with—and made her head feel as if it would explode.

Elise knew her face contorted with pain and the effort to subdue it, but still she would not retreat. "Then tell me. Where do you know me from? When?"

His hands fell away, his face stricken—whether because of her questions or the realization that she was suffering right now, she couldn't tell. And she didn't care, if it gave her the advantage. He ran his fingers through his hair. "Believe me, Elise," he finally said, "I would tell you every detail about us if I thought it would help."

She knew she had the upper hand now, so she pressed on. "But it won't help your claim, will it? In fact, it'll hurt you because I still won't know you!"

"I don't know that, but I'm very afraid you won't."

"And why won't I know you?" she persisted, trying to get him to give in, to catch him in his own preposterous reasoning.

"I don't know that either," he murmured. "But I intend to find out."

His determination stalled her attack. Was this the threat, then, that she'd sensed earlier?

Damn him, but it was hard to retain any certainty when faced with such conviction! *Was* there some way she could have once known this man? But how could she, and forget him? It wasn't as if he were an acquaintance who'd passed through her life and so was easily overlooked. By his claim, they had loved each other. Deeply. Intimately.

The pressure in her head reached a crushing intensity. She swayed.

"Elise!" Dylan grasped her arm to steady her. "My God, you're white as a sheet! We've got to get you to a doctor."

"You think I haven't been seeing one?" she asked, fighting down nausea, fighting back tears of frustration. Because of this pain, she'd lose her battle with this man. She swallowed with difficulty and gave in. "I don't need this. I don't need this kind of uproar in my life. It can't be doing me any good."

"Ellie—"

"Let me go. Now."

Dylan stepped back. Finding her way to the street unobstructed, Elise staggered to the opening. She wanted to be shed of him now that she had the chance, but her legs felt perilously weak, and she paused a moment to regain her equilibrium.

She leaned against the wall, inhaling large draughts of air and turning her face upward toward the meager light as a flower would seek the sun. Her nausea abated and she felt better. Elise remembered the gallery's ledgers.

Let them rot, she thought, but then she heard a rustle of papers behind her. She turned. Dylan's large form crouched as he scooped up the papers, arranging them so they all lay lengthwise. He gave them a last squaring up before he placed them in the sack, resting them against the side that was still intact. He rose and handed the bundle to her. Elise took it, hugging it to her as she peered at him through her tunneled vision.

Dylan Colman. The name still rang no bells in her head nor in her heart. With the light behind her, she now had the advantage of being able to study him while concealing her own features. His skin was as pale as it had been this afternoon, although now two wedges of color whetted the razor's edge of his cheekbones. The nostrils of his bladelike nose flared with barely manageable emotion as he regarded her. He was an extremely striking man. Beyond handsomeness, though, Elise realized, he had a definite presence. She'd met few people who had that quality. They drew every gaze when they entered a room. Their light burned brightly within them, radiating an aura of specialness and influence that attracted others to them like moths to flame.

There was no way on earth she could have forgotten this man.

As before, he stood with his hands buried in his coat pockets in a manner that implied suppressed urgency. *He loves me,* she thought. And it would cost him greatly to let her walk away right now. His black eyes were inscrutable, his sensual lips sculpted downward in a pensive frown. He looked discouraged but not defeated, although Elise realized that indeed she had won a victory of some kind. They'd engaged in a battle of wills: he'd wanted her to admit recognition and she had not done it. But he meant to do everything in his power to make her do so.

Elise wondered what kept her from putting as much space as possible between them.

"Look, Dylan—" she said and stopped, startled. On her lips, his name did evoke a familiar essence. Without hesitation, she rejected the sensation. It was nothing more than the power of suggestion, a pseudo-brainwashing tactic of asking the same question over and over until one got the "correct" answer.

But you want answers, too.

God, she would go crazy if she allowed herself to continue this way, wondering about every insubstantial flash of intuition, real or imagined, that struck her.

"Dylan," she repeated firmly, "I don't know how you know those things about me. But let's just choose to believe, for one moment, that we knew each other once and I've simply forgotten you. The fact remains that I don't know you now. You are a stranger to me." Why did saying these things make her want to cry? "I'm sorry to have to tell you this, because it's obvious you feel we shared a great passion. But I don't love you."

He said nothing, only looked at her implacably. His attitude plainly said that he wouldn't argue, but neither would he agree.

It doesn't matter, Elise thought. She didn't have to convince him of anything, either. "So. Now that we've established that you've no reason to stay, you can leave town, right?"

Dylan turned his head and regarded the side of the building dispassionately. A muscle leapt in his jaw. "I'm not going anywhere, Elise."

"I beg your pardon?"

"I'm staying here in Viento Blanco." He drew a deep breath, once again fixing that unwavering gaze upon her. "I intend to make you remember me, Elise. I won't...I can't leave until I do."

She stared at him. "You have no right to disrupt my life with your outrageous stories about long-lost love!" She thought wildly for a means to convince him he couldn't continue to torment her. "I wasn't kidding about the police, you know. You've accosted me twice now. They'll slap a restraining order on you if they don't run you out of town first. And Keith—"

"Yes, Keith," Dylan interrupted, his voice deadly soft. "The man you're going to marry. You've made it clear you don't love me, but can you honestly say you love him, Elise?"

"Of all the—"

"Do you?"

"It's none of your business!"

"Fine. It wasn't a trick question, but I believe I got the answer I needed."

"Have you, then?" She felt her face flush with indignation. His unyielding certitude inflamed her, banished the cold from her body, cleared her battered brain. So he thought it indisputable that her past was linked with his, and that he held her fate in his hands. The rebelliousness she'd felt earlier returned in force, and Elise searched her mind for a way to challenge this man. Because he didn't own her or her past.

"Well, let me tell you how much good that answer will do you," she said. "In five days I'm marrying Keith Hurston. And nothing you intend or do or think will matter."

She saw him take her statement like a blow to the solar plexus. Yes, she had satisfaction, but it was a dubious triumph as she watched shock hit him like a bullet, and she knew she'd fired the shot. His handsome face drained of color, his black eyes burning within their sockets like two holes.

"No!" he cried and took a step toward her.

This time Elise didn't hesitate but turned and ran. She didn't need an ounce of intuition to tell her that, with her revelation, Dylan Colman would have held her until he'd used every method within his power to make her his again.

His fist crashed into the brick wall. Blessed pain shot up his arm and brought him back to sanity. Yet reality still hovered out of reach. He simply could not believe this was happening.

She didn't love him. It almost made the not-remembering-him part anticlimactic—except for the fact she was marrying another man within the week. Nothing could top that.

He felt such anger at that moment, at himself for not meaning enough to Elise for her to remember him, at Elise herself for not wanting to search the darkest corners of her consciousness and remember. It was irrational anger, he realized, for this whole mess wasn't her fault. It didn't seem that she'd deliberately disappeared or intentionally forgotten him. No, she hadn't asked to forget anything, nor to nearly die, nor to go on hurting as she did. Obviously, the pain was barely tolerable. It almost killed him to see her in such agony. And he was beginning to understand he only caused her more pain. Even so, it still seemed as if she'd taken what he'd thought was a timeless experience and just...dismissed it. *We don't even have the memories,* he thought cynically.

And then there was Keith Hurston. There wasn't the slightest possibility that she loved him, not the way that Dylan knew she could love. Not the way he *knew* she loved him.

He saw it in her face, how she fought it, fought the instances of recognition that hit her, that flashed across her features with the speed of a nerve synapse. He wanted to answer all of her questions, to tell her how and when they knew each other, but what if such details sparked nothing in her mind? Somewhere among her possessions, she must have some tangible reminder of him, and if that hadn't already produced a flicker... God help him, he didn't think he could endure it, to have the memories that had given his life meaning reduced to so much dust, forever lost on the wind.

It was downright freaky how things had happened, how events had plotted to keep them apart.

Dylan stepped from his place between the buildings. The street was as desolate and dismal as a ghost town. He'd seen a smattering of inns and motels along the highway as he'd entered Viento Blanco from the north this afternoon. However, he had no desire to sample the accommodations here. This burg and its mummifying fog were getting to him. He'd head inland. It was no more than twenty, twenty-five miles to Healdsburg or Santa Rosa. Perhaps if he got away from this eerie atmosphere, his thoughts would fall into perspective and the situation would lose its outlandishness. Who knew? Maybe tomorrow he'd wake up and find it was all a bad dream, that Elise Nash loved him.

But she didn't love him. The impossibility of it struck him anew. He set his jaw and pushed through the fog toward his car.

No, she didn't love him now, but she had done so once. She would again.

Chapter Three

Elise entered the house and swept through the enclosed porch to the kitchen, bringing the chill with her. It quickly disappeared in the warmth of the kitchen.

"Aunt Char?" she called, setting her armful of papers on the counter.

"Elise?" came the wavering reply from the other room. Aunt Charlotte appeared at the kitchen doorway. Her face shone with relief. "Oh, thank goodness you're back!"

Elise spread her arms and looked down at herself. "All in one piece. I told you you'd nothing to worry about." She prayed her face wouldn't show the tumult whirling through her and that her hands didn't shake.

"Yes, well, you left so long ago."

Elise glanced at the clock. "It's only been half an hour," she said, getting that sense of imprisonment again, despite her own relief at making it safely home. She gestured toward the untidy pile of ledgers. "I would have been back sooner but I stuffed this bag too full and it ripped open about halfway home. Heavens, I'm starved!" she rushed on, divesting herself of her coat and chafing her arms.

Aunt Charlotte took the bait, bustling past Elise to the stove. "Let's get some of this hot soup into you. 'Sakes, I can't imagine why you'd want to be out on a night like this for any reason."

Neither can I, Elise silently agreed, trying to put the image of implacable black eyes out of her mind.

She succeeded, to a degree, as she and Charlotte ate, and later when Keith arrived. The warm soup did indeed oust the cold, as did the bright conversation that followed—made brighter by both Keith and Charlotte trying, obviously for Elise's sake, to downplay the afternoon's events.

Keith allayed any lingering worries her aunt might have had with chitchat about his and Elise's upcoming wedding. Though Elise had insisted that they keep it to a small ceremony at the justice of the peace's office, followed by an informal reception here, her aunt's anticipation ran so high they could have been planning the social event of the season. Elise was glad to bring her aunt joy instead of worry for once. As Charlotte chattered on about cakes and flowers, Elise felt her nerves settle, the cottony sensation in her head dwindled and she allowed her mind to wander.

At times, within the security of her aunt's snug home, Elise felt almost healthy. Almost normal; enough so to feel restlessly confined in a diametrical effect that pushed and pulled at her. The infirmities that continued to plague her would begin to seem less restrictive, much as the influence of the fog was temporarily stanched by a crackling fire or a cheerfully lit room. In the past month—one in which she'd made the most progress toward recovery—Elise found she had to fight against depending too much on this false sense of well-being. She would never regain her full strength by limiting herself to only those surroundings that provided comfort. *No pain, no gain,* wasn't that the saying?

But to have no place to venture except into the stultifying fog that hung over Viento Blanco. She realized, now that she'd experienced true deprivation, that she was definitely one of those people whose moods were influenced by the weather. Elise longed for even a glimpse of the sun. She wanted to feel it kiss her skin, she wanted so badly to bake under it she couldn't imagine ever getting too much. She wished for a place where it was possible to try.

You've got to get away.

The compulsion came over her all of a sudden, making her take a quick breath that drew both Keith's and Charlotte's attention.

"Are you all right, dear?" her aunt asked in a contrite tone that told Elise Keith had done his job. Charlotte had obviously forgotten all about the threat of the stranger and was now feeling a little ashamed for not being more attentive to Elise's state of mind.

"I'm fine, Aunt Char," she answered with a smile. "But I am a little tired."

Dear man that he was, Keith picked up his cue. "I should be getting home," he said, rising from his place on the couch next to Elise. He held out a hand to her. "Walk me to the door?"

She rose and, arms linked about each other's waist, they walked to the foyer beyond the living room. There, he turned her into his embrace. Elise rested her cheek on his shoulder, drawing comfort from him as she had so many times since her accident.

Maybe her impulse to get away wasn't so very odd. The two of them had decided to forgo a honeymoon until she was completely recovered, but perhaps a few weeks in the sun was just what she needed.

Yet they *were* going away, and it occurred to her how irrational her notion had been earlier to postpone the wedding. Next week Keith had an industry conference at Asilomar, near Carmel, at which he intended to show off his new wife. How had she forgotten something so important to him? Most likely it was because a trip to Monterey Bay, with its equally intrusive fog, represented no change of venue in her mind.

No change at all in her life.

Avoiding that thought, Elise snuggled closer to Keith, lifting her head to meet his good-night kiss. Here, too, was the warmth she sought, though it struck her that it wasn't enough either. It—he?—would never be enough. She pressed closer to him still, again trying to elude such fatalistic thoughts. Hadn't she found so much else with this man to compensate for anything that might be missing? Did it count for nothing that he'd stood by her, stayed with her through a hell of physical and emotional anguish?

Can you honestly say you love him? The words, spoken by her tall, dark stranger, leapt to mind.

True, Keith wasn't the man of her dreams, but how often did any person end up sharing their life with the perfect mate? A woman could make herself very unhappy wishing and waiting for something more. Wanting something more. It was better to find someone with similar tastes and background and complementary goals. These were the qualities that provided the fertile ground in which true love would grow. Romantic love, passionate love was a hothouse flower, glorious and intense in the height of its bloom, but fading quickly.

What Keith had done for her *did* count, she thought fiercely, more than anything else could. Not for the first time, Elise wondered what she'd have done without Keith Hurston. She couldn't imagine where she'd be right now.

Far, far away from Viento Blanco came the answer.

Abruptly, she broke the kiss.

Keith peered down at her. "Are you sure you're all right?" he asked.

Elise nodded, avoiding his eyes lest he spot the clashing emotions in hers. She had a strong feeling that something vital hinged on her maintaining an appearance of complete composure with Keith. Something as vital as what little freedom she had right now.

"I talked to Sheriff Roswell about that guy," he said when she didn't answer. "Frank said he'd keep an eye out himself. They're on a reduced staff right now, you know, until high season. But that means anyone out of the ordinary will be that much easier to spot. You'll let me know, though, if you see him around, won't you?"

"Of—of course," Elise stammered, hating herself for lying. But she couldn't tell Keith about her latest encounter with Dylan. Why, though? Why protect him, a man who made untenable assertions, who seemed driven by events that had unfolded in an entirely different world?

Because. You want answers.

"You're sure you don't know him?" Keith said, his voice again taking on a tinge of skepticism, the faintly accusing tone that irritated her as it had earlier today. Though his suspicions weren't, she had to admit, entirely without foundation, still he needed to trust her judgment.

From somewhere, she found the mastery over her conflicting thoughts that enabled her to look him in the eye and say with conviction, "I'm positive."

Regardless of her reasoning, it was another lie.

She tried to neutralize her culpability with a smile of thanks. "I do appreciate your taking care of this matter."

"Sure, sweetheart," he said, then frowned in concern. "I wish I didn't have to spend the rest of the week at my Santa Rosa office, but I've got some business there that just can't be put off. Especially if I expect to take time on Thursday to drive you to your doctor's appointment in San Francisco."

Guilt continued to goad her for the ungrateful thoughts of a moment before. Keith was so conscientious, so accommodating of her. "I hate being such a burden," she apologized. "I really haven't made an effort to get over my phobia about driving."

Yes, here was yet another area of avoidance in her life. They seemed to be coming out of the woodwork today.

"Nonsense," Keith assured her, "you're anything but a burden. Besides, Dr. Emerson said it was perfectly normal for you to be reluctant to get behind the wheel again after your accident."

"We're not talking about reluctance, Keith. We're talking about sheer terror."

"And it's *normal* sheer terror. Not unreasonable and not irrational. But if your apprehension is annoying you, maybe that means psychologically you're now ready to deal with the issue. Why don't you talk to Dr. Emerson about it Thursday?''

Elise was surprised and pleased by his suggestion. Much of his recent support had been through tempering her impatience, cautioning her not to try too much too soon. She knew that he liked taking care of her, perhaps more than he should, more than she should allow.

Yet what he said made utter sense. That was it, the reason she was feeling so restless and discontented, why her headaches had returned. She *was* ready to move on, was perfectly capable of doing so, though she might have latent doubts and hesitations. It was natural for her to fight progress, just as it was natural for her to yearn for it.

"I think I will talk to Dr. Emerson about it." She gazed up at him. "I knew there was a reason I said I'd marry you," she vowed with a hint of a flirtatious smile.

He caught her chin between his thumb and index finger. He wasn't smiling. "Just don't forget it, Elise." Then the smile came, one that both reassured and disturbed her.

"I've been wondering, Keith," she said, dropping her gaze yet again, "would you ever leave Viento Blanco?" She was thinking about the cabin, trying to imagine them both there. No images came to mind.

"Leave? Is that what's frightening you, darling?"

She started to shake her head when something stopped her. Was it?

"Well, I'm here to stay," Keith went on without waiting for her response. "You're stuck with me, I'm afraid."

It wasn't what she'd meant, but the answer seemed to suffice.

After Keith left, Elise returned to the living room. There she found Aunt Charlotte still sitting under a cloud of self-reproach.

"I'm sorry, Elise," she said. "I should have remembered your having that frightening experience today. I'm afraid it just went straight out of my head. But you were acting so normal," she defended herself.

"I *am* normal, Aunt Char," Elise said with a new certainty. She dropped onto the sofa with a sigh. "And not a bit tired, all of a sudden." She wrinkled her nose. "I do not, however, feel like tackling those books tonight."

"That reminds me!" Charlotte spoke up. "You know all those boxes Keith brought back from your studio in Oregon? The ones in the attic?"

"I know *of* them," Elise teased, sinking more comfortably into the cushions, "though I've never actually made their acquaintance."

"Oh, you." Even at seventy-six, Charlotte Nash could dimple like a girl. "I merely thought you might want to go through them before the ceremony on Saturday. I know that horrid landlord of yours sold your furniture, but he couldn't have gotten rid of everything a bride might need in a new home."

Elise's sense of well-being deflated slightly. She studied her folded hands and wondered why her aunt's innocuous suggestion produced a new crop of anxieties in her. "I'm sure Keith has every manner of kitchen appliance we'd ever need, Aunt Char."

"A bachelor like him?"

"He's hardly your typical bachelor," Elise reminded her. "Keith's divorce left him with everything, including the blender and Crockpot."

"Oh, that's right," Charlotte said. "I forgot."

Elise, too, often forgot about Keith's brief first marriage. He rarely spoke of his ex-wife, though when he did it was with a bitterness she rarely saw in her imperturbable fiancé. From what Elise could gather, the woman had found Viento Blanco too confining, the choice of diversion too limited, and had left him to move south for the more vigorous pace of life. Keith had apparently had no clue she was unhappy. And there'd been no talk of compromise. She just left. Such rejection would leave any man bitter.

Why did you disappear without a word?

It was another of Dylan's questions, Elise realized with a start—asked of her. He could follow her even here, it seemed.

"Then it's your gain and that foolish woman's loss," her aunt said loyally. "She must have been very selfish to leave such a fine man."

Elise was surprised to find herself shaking her head slowly. "Not necessarily. Viento Blanco isn't for everyone."

"Well." Aunt Charlotte rose, grasping the snug side seams at her hips and giving her dress a tug southward. "You never know what you might find in those boxes that you could use. Aren't your art supplies in them?"

"Yes," Elise answered.

"There you are!" Aunt Charlotte exclaimed triumphantly. "You can go through them to see what's missing and order anything you need to start painting again."

"You're right," Elise agreed firmly. Though it was normal to resist change, normal to want to remain in a secure place, she needed to push herself. "And anything I don't need, I should get rid of. I can't clutter up your house forever."

"Darling, I wasn't suggesting...I only want for you what will make you happy. You deserve to be, dear child, after all you've been through. Sometimes I wish I could do more... You're not cluttering my house," Charlotte protested. "You never could."

But Elise knew she was—her presence here disrupted more than her aunt's home and routine. It was her emotional needs that upset Charlotte, because her aunt had never been able to meet them and knew she never could. Elise loved her aunt dearly and knew Charlotte loved her as well, but there was something absent from their relationship, something Elise had missed since her parents died—a basic need for that unbreakable bond of kinship, of family. Of marriage. A permanence reassuring her that regardless of where she went in the world, there was someone who thought of her and missed her and longed for her to come back to him.

You expect too much of people, she told herself as she had countless times before.

Elise glanced up to find her aunt looking at her in expectation. "I'm sorry, Aunt Char. Did you say something?"

Charlotte smiled her sweet, simple smile. "I know you'll be busy after the wedding, but I was so hoping I could ask you to do a small landscape for that wall in my bedroom."

It was Aunt Char's way of telling Elise she *was* wanted and needed. She stood and gave the older woman a hug. Against hers, Charlotte's cheek had the soft, smooth texture of elderly skin, conjuring up memories of grandparents long passed away and producing in Elise a thread of the very connection she'd been seeking. "Of course," she said. "Anything for you, dear."

They decided to call it an early night and together went up the stairs to their bedrooms. At the end of the dimly lit hallway, Elise spotted the door to the attic stairs. And at the top of them lay the sum of her life's possessions. She made a mental resolution to sort through them before Saturday, apprehensions aside. It was perfectly natural, she told herself, that there'd be a lot in those boxes she'd rather not have to make decisions about—keep or throw, sell or donate. She'd just have to deal with that aspect of the situation. On the positive side, she could make a list, as Aunt Charlotte suggested, of what was missing and what she'd need.

Elise realized she would even do it gladly—if she really thought she'd find what was missing. Or what she needed.

Elise was in the back room of the gallery the next day when she heard the bells on the door signal the arrival of a potential customer.

Except as she entered the main gallery she saw it wasn't someone looking for that one particular painting.

It was Dylan Colman. Looking for her.

He stood just inside the doorway. Again, he had on that long oilskin duster, though under it today he wore a tan crewneck sweater and slacks. Certainly an improvement over the brooding all-black attire of yesterday. Still, it seemed no less portentous.

Behind her back, Elise gripped one wrist in her other hand to hide the sudden tension that rose up in her at his appearance. *You can handle this,* she told herself. She didn't shirk his unsmiling gaze but eyed him warily.

"I gather you're not surprised to see me," he said after a moment.

"No, I'm not."

"I can't help but find that encouraging."

"I don't know why you would."

He took a step forward and set a large basket, its contents hidden by a white linen napkin, on the counter. "Because if you truly believed I was a danger to you, you wouldn't be here. Alone."

His emphasis on the last word did indeed escalate her apprehension. Again, she felt no sense of physical threat from this man—more a psychological one. There was a cat-and-mouse quality to today's conversation, in the way he watched her. She had to remember that he couldn't make her believe anything she didn't want to. He could have no power over her if she wouldn't give it to him.

Elise made herself shrug nonchalantly. "I wouldn't be so sure of myself if I were you."

"Why?" He glanced around. "Aren't you alone?"

She was mindful not to answer that question. Let him wonder. "I only meant the police have an eye out for you. Keith does, too."

"Ah." He sank his hands into his pockets and sauntered, seemingly without deliberation, closer to her. Yet the movement brought him farther into the gallery and away from the window where he could be easily seen. "I'll take my chances with the police," he murmured. "As for Mr. Hurston, I believe he's out of town most days."

Your move, she could almost hear him say. Nothing was stopping her from going closer to the window where *she* could be seen more readily. As casually as possible, Elise drifted toward the front of the gallery, though her route brought her close to Dylan as she brushed past him. Still watching her, he made no move, yet she had the oddest sensation that an energy—like a magnetic field—surrounded him, its influence increasing and diminishing in connection with her proximity to him. It raised the fine hairs on the back of her neck as it had last night and made her feel weaker. She fought down a surge of alarm.

"Of course you'd know Keith's whereabouts as well as mine," she said. "Big Brother is watching, apparently."

"I see. You've reasoned it all out, then—you think I'm with the government. Privy to dossiers and records, all sorts of information obtained through all sorts of methods."

His inflection was chiding, and Elise couldn't help her reaction. "It's not out of the realm of possibility," she challenged.

Dylan lifted one brow skeptically. "No. It's as likely an explanation as any. Not so terribly far from the truth, if you must know. But however I garnered my information, that doesn't explain everything, because the question still is, why would I care, Elise?"

"I don't know!" Pain flashed like wildfire along the side of her head. Closing her eyes, Elise pressed the pads of her fingers against her temple. He was getting to her, and she'd vowed he wouldn't.

She heard him make a sound of disgust, and she forced her eyes open. It didn't seem he was disgusted with her, however. No, she noticed, curiously, his mouth had tightened in self-loathing.

"I brought food," Dylan announced.

"Food?" she echoed, baffled. What *was* his game?

"Yes, food." He lifted the napkin and peered into the basket. "I have smoked salmon and capers. Sliced avocado. Wedges of lime to squeeze over it." He ticked off items with a staccato shortness, and she wondered at the unidentifiable aspect in his tone. "You wouldn't believe how difficult it was for me to find a decent clam chowder, but I know you love it. Damn if I could find fresh *pico de gallo,* though, in this godforsaken area."

In spite of herself, Elise stepped closer to the counter and gaped at the contents of the basket as Dylan went on, "I apologize if the assortment seems eclectic, but I wanted to bring you your favorites."

Elise switched her gaze to him. "How did you—" She stopped herself. Futility. That's what she heard in his voice. So—was he giving up on convincing her of his tall tale about the two of them? Why did the possibility that he might be fill her with disappointment?

"You're guessing again," she said.

"How could I be guessing, Elise?" he demanded. "These are your favorite foods, aren't they?"

"Somehow you found out I grew up in the Boston area, that I lived here in Viento Blanco till I graduated high school, that I went to college and lived in the Pacific Northwest." She dismissed the basket and its contents with her hand. "Anyone could ferret out those details and come to conclusions about my tastes in food."

"Is that right?" he asked angrily. He closed his eyes, an apparent bid for control. Then he opened them, those bottomless black eyes boring into her. "Tell me, then, how I know your favorite colors are blue, like the sky, and deep forest green? How would I know that even though you're an artist you still believe that no painting or sculpture or rendering could ever surpass the beauty of nature? Yes, Elise," he rushed on, forestalling her further outburst of cynicism, "I know that for a creative type, you consider yourself quite good with numbers. But even when you deal with mathematics, you can't prevent your imagination from taking over."

She stiffened. "I don't know what you're talking about."

"I think you do. You think the number one is stuffy. Condescending. Six has an inferiority complex, being between the easily divisible five and lucky seven. Two is simple hearted. And three is like... How did you put it? Like the Mother Earth, life-giving."

Elise stared at him. She would have laughed at him, trying to convince her by relating her personality analysis of numbers, had he not been so dead-on serious. Or dead-on right.

Her head was throbbing now, but she found the pain secondary to the confoundedness of this man's knowledge. She'd never told anyone such whimsical thoughts, had barely isolated them from the millions of impressions that went in and out of her head each day. Yet this was soul-deep stuff. And he knew it.

Dylan must have seen comprehension dawning on her face and feared she'd turn from it yet again, for he reached out to grasp her shoulders, holding her fast. "You want children, Elise. Lots of them, so your sons and daughters will always have someone to love them long after you're gone."

His gaze gentled then, his voice growing rough with emotion. "You feel things so deeply, Elise. So passionately. You can't stop yourself from being that way, in everything you do. You've got such a well of compassion for others in you, your instincts to protect are incredible. You've a strong commitment to preserving wildlife and half believe that—" strangely, he faltered a moment, as if struck by a realization himself "—that in ... another life you were a wild animal, small and quick, but unfortunately not quick enough."

A trembling started in her, radiating outward from her core. Elise realized she'd stared so long without blinking that her eyes had begun to water. "How do you know these things?" she cried.

"You told me, Ellie," he answered raggedly, a profound weariness in his eyes. "You told me everything."

A lightning bolt of sheer agony hit her. Elise gasped, her knees buckling, hands grasping blindly for support. Dylan gathered her against him, and she buried her face in his chest as she forgot about fighting this man and instead focused every ounce of her strength on fighting the torment in her brain. She clutched the front of his sweater, struggling for control over her own body. Pain assaulted her in wave upon wave, yet within the circle of Dylan's arms, she found cover from the worst of it. Within the circumference of the energy she'd felt emanating from him, she was protected rather than threatened. Desperate for relief, Elise finally let go of her resistance, let down her own barriers, and let that force fight her battle for her. And amazingly the pain eased to a tolerable level.

She floated on the ebb of that sweet release for several minutes. Then slowly, as if she rose from a great depth, she became aware of Dylan's voice. He didn't seem to be talking to her, though.

"God help me, what am I doing?" he asked in a tortured whisper. "How can I do this to you? You're so fragile..." His arms tightened, bringing her farther into the circle of his protection. "There's got to be a way..."

Elise remained silent, wanting nothing to disturb the peace she felt—or to provoke that terrible pain again. More minutes passed before a gentle hand lifted her chin and Elise found herself looking into Dylan's black eyes, now liquid, caressing.

"*Do* you believe in reincarnation, Elise?" he asked. "That the same soul can be born, live and die over and over again on a quest for perfection? That we encounter other souls in our travels to whom we become linked forever by experience, by love?"

Elise blinked, wondering if she heard him right. "You can't be suggesting—"

"How can you explain my knowing you?" His eyes searched the depths of hers. "You tell me, Ellie. *Is* there another explanation?"

She shook her head dumbly, mindless of the ache that still pulsed dully in her brain. Because what he *was* suggesting was incredible.

"Ellie, please. Think about it for a minute. Even if you don't remember me, can you deny that I've known you before? No," he said quickly as she made a move to pull away from him. "I'm not asking you to remember me. I can't torture you like that. And I'm not some crazy, dangerous madman out to get you. But please believe, just for a moment, what I'm saying—we two have shared a lifetime of love. Does it seem so impossible to you?''

Did it? No denying it, he knew her. This wasn't lies or threats or vague allusions. This was as real and as certain and as vivid as nothing had been to her in ages. But had they loved each other? Elise closed her eyes and struggled with the magnitude of so great a love. Even in a thousand lifetimes, it was a rare experience. If they had loved each other so much, *why had she forgotten it?*

Was this what was missing? The vital jigsaw piece that, when added to her jumbled life, would cause all the other elements to fall into place and magically disclose the whole picture? Did this man have the answers she'd been searching for?

Was *she* the one who was giving up? Elise wondered. Was she so worn down by the fruitlessness of her quest that she'd become one of those people who looked for miracle cures, any avenue of pursuit that might keep hope alive?

And yet...she'd been focusing her energies on moving forward and making a new life with Keith. She'd looked to the future, believing that was where her recovery lay, believing nothing good could come from dredging up the painful past. But maybe she'd been wrong—perhaps the key to regaining wholeness lay in the past.

A past as unknown to her as the future. As was this man. Impossible? She gazed up at him and was struck anew by the total conviction in his eyes. If anyone could have traversed time and space to find her, Dylan Colman was that man.

Despite herself, Elise tried to conjure up the brief recognition she'd experienced, when Dylan had kissed her yesterday, that might substantiate his story. It occurred to her now that it hadn't been recognition. Instead, it had been a connection: a piece of each of them had indeed fit together—not because they'd done so before, but possibly because they were designed to do so. What was that, if not kismet?

"If...I were to believe you," Elise said slowly, "that we once knew and loved each other, what would that change now?"

At her words, Dylan rested his forehead against hers in relief. In thanks, almost. He gave a dry chuckle. "To tell the truth, I hadn't thought that far." He hesitated. "You might consider putting off your wedding until we've figured it out."

Elise drew away from him and wrapped her arms about herself in an attempt to retain the fortitude his embrace had provided her. Hadn't she considered the same option? "And what would I say to Keith?"

"I don't know," said Dylan. *I don't care,* said his tone, not quite insulting. "I can't help thinking that if you truly felt he was your life mate, you wouldn't have any doubts. But you are questioning yourself."

"*You're* questioning me, pushing me!" She wasn't surprised when her head began to pulsate again. "Keith Hurston's given me nothing but love and support. He stood beside me through months of suffering, when I could only take his help and comfort and give nothing back."

"I understand why you care for him, Elise, why you think you owe him your loyalty. But do you love him? Tell me you do, and I'll leave right now."

"I—" The words stuck in her throat, and she realized it was in part because she didn't want to see Dylan Colman walk out of her life. Not until she got the answers *she* wanted. And she desperately wanted answers—more than she wanted what Keith Hurston provided her.

Do you love him? the question pricked her, demanded a response.

"How could I...how could I not?" she whispered, squeezing her eyes shut to drive back the bite of pain, but it was too aggressive.

Anger helps, she remembered. Perhaps because she had a right to feel anger—or a need to be angry, as a step in the healing process. But anger at what, whom? Not Keith or Aunt Charlotte. At fate, perhaps, for putting her through such an onerous trial, one she couldn't possibly have done anything to deserve in this lifetime—or in the last.

Or had she?

Elise opened her eyes and found Dylan observing her. He was so handsome, so potent, so powerful, in a way that didn't belong here in Viento Blanco, or even to this time. In a way that couldn't belong to her, Elise Nash, the woman she was today.

Fate. Kismet. Karma. Had it torn their two souls apart for a reason? What *had* she done?

No. What had he done?

"This is absolute lunacy," she muttered. She sank into a nearby chair, too weary to continue holding off the freight train bent on roaring through her brain. It was a kind of relief, in fact. Numbing.

"I can't...lay blame," she said through a haze, "just to find an answer. A reason why...or how this happened to me." Her throat constricted with her frustration. "It's not right. It's nothing I did." Tears gathered in the corners of her eyes. *I must believe that.* "But somehow...I've got to find a way to stop this...aching."

Though her vision had gone dim around the edges, Elise registered the worried expression on Dylan's face as he squatted in front of her and took her hands.

"Shh," he soothed her, chafing her fingers against his. "All right, no more, love. No more pushing, I promise. Don't think of it now. We'll find a way, don't worry. Relax, take a deep breath for me. That's it. One more."

Elise did as he directed, tried to suspend her thoughts, to keep them from going backward or forward. It helped. Her vision cleared. Still crouched before her, Dylan gazed up at her. "Better?" he asked.

"Yes."

He remained where he was, bent legs spread with her knees between them, her fingers held loosely in his as his thumbs kneaded the backs of her hands. At this moment, he seemed anything but a danger.

In fact, as his gaze held hers, Elise discovered something there: he was aching, too—aching for her pain, certainly, but also aching with questions. It struck her that, if she were to believe his story, he must be feeling much the same as she did right now: confused to the bone by events that had literally ripped his world apart, frustrated by a maze of inconsistencies and altered facts that should have been irrefutable. And anger. She could see that Dylan was angry, too. This shouldn't have happened to either one of them.

Though neither of them so much as blinked, Elise detected a change in her connection with this man. Indeed, she had been brought into a circle of certain truths. They'd established a set of givens that, though still unexplainable, were at least conceded as such. And she now looked out at the world from within that circle, with Dylan. He wanted answers, too, and the goal formed an unspoken bond between them. One that by default pitted everyone else against them.

Elise tore her gaze away from his. The clock on the wall told her it was almost two. Keith had said he'd be back in Viento Blanco by midafternoon.

"You'd better go," she murmured, not meeting Dylan's eyes.

He apparently understood her inflection, for he gave her fingers a final squeeze and stood. "All right. I'll be back tomorrow, though."

Now was her chance to protest, to again claim he had no right to intrude on her life, to assure him that the authorities or Keith would never permit it. But Elise was silent.

Dylan left the basket.

She clasped her hands, pressing her thumbs against her lips as she sat in thought. Yes, she wanted to know what he knew about her, but she had a way to go toward believing him. Still, a line had been strung across the chasm yawning between the known and the unknown, a tightrope she must negotiate with extreme caution if she were to make it to the other side and find the answers she sought. And she had to try to find them. It was time.

But she would have to be careful with this man. The danger was still there, for she'd seen something else in his eyes: a desperation that rivaled her own.

As soon as he could, Dylan cut off of Seaspray Avenue onto a side street. Not that there was a single person in sight. But who knew if one of the other shopkeepers had seen him come out of the gallery. He didn't want to take a chance of Hurston being alerted, not only for Dylan's own purposes, but for Elise's protection as well.

What had he done? How could he have told her the things he had, suggested what he had? Raised a thousand more doubts about him in her mind? Elise was right: it was absolute lunacy to think she would believe him.

But she had. Or at least he'd given her a reason to want to believe. Dylan knew he'd made a breakthrough. What he did next was crucial. He already saw that pushing her didn't help. It hurt, both Elise and himself, and more than just physically. Even if it cut into her resistance, he couldn't bear putting her through such torture. Still, he couldn't very well deny the urgency of the situation. As yet, Elise hadn't been given a strong enough reason not to proceed with her wedding. He took what comfort he could from the fact that she'd not professed love for Hurston. That, Dylan concluded, would have killed him.

No, it wasn't love that bound her to Hurston, but it was something strong and powerful, nonetheless. Something that prevented her from remembering. Something that prevented her from loving him, Dylan.

The conclusion made him pause just as he reached his car. Perhaps the key lay not in making her remember—not yet. *Don't ask that of her, especially since it causes her so much anguish and pain.* But if he could at least lay a coat of doubt over her relationship with Hurston, she wouldn't need to remember the past they'd shared to call off her wedding.

It wasn't enough, Dylan realized. He needed more than doubt. Actually, he needed to eliminate it, once and for all, because he had to go back, within days. And since he needed to take her with him as his wife, he needed her to love him again—without the doubts that had kept them apart the first time.

Was it possible in so short a time? It'd happened the very same way, over a few weeks of sun, sailing and loving. Maybe by taking her down the same path of getting to know each other, she'd fall in love with him. And then, perhaps, she'd remember.

Would lightning strike twice, though? Had it struck even once? For obviously something had provided her with a reservation to keep her from coming with him once before. And Elise was now in a different place, both literally and figuratively, than that time. A place that put her even farther away from him. She had two powerful incentives—her health and Keith Hurston—to resist Dylan. Yet he had to believe there was a chance. It *had* happened before, and it would again. It was just a matter of time.

And time, thought Dylan Colman, was something he had very little of.

Chapter Four

He kept his promise. He came back.

Elise stood at the gallery's dutch door, its upper half open for the first time this spring, and watched Dylan striding up the cobbled street toward her. The breeze coming through the doorway was crisp and strong but welcome, for it was responsible for sweeping away the fog and providing the first sunny day Elise had experienced since returning to Viento Blanco. The brilliant sunlight cleansed the town like a miracle cure, changing the whole aspect of Seaspray Avenue. The colorful storefronts perked up like flowers after a good rain; the windows shone proudly, having for once the opportunity to reflect something of significance. Indeed, her spirit seemed unburdened of its troubles, as if nothing, not even the mysterious darkness that surrounded Dylan Colman, could hold its own against a radiant force that saw everything, knew everything.

He wore jeans today and a dark green windbreaker unzipped halfway to reveal a pale blue sweater. Combined with the leather deck shoes on his feet, the clothes made him look the epitome of approachable casualness. Still, Elise noticed, nothing could be called ordinary about this man.

The corners of his mouth lifted in greeting as he stopped just outside the door, and Elise couldn't prevent her own smile of gladness—for the gift of this day, naturally, but also, she realized, at seeing him again. She'd be fooling herself not to admit she was relieved he kept his word, for his appearance in town still held a surreal quality for her. When she awoke this morning, she half expected Dylan Colman to be part of a vivid dream.

"Is this the 'white wind' Viento Blanco's named for?" he asked as the breeze ruffled his hair, the sunlight spangling it through a lattice of branches. Black brows jutted over his deep-set eyes, shading them from the unique brightness. His gaze was as warming as the sun as it flitted over her, lashes flickering in a discreet perusal that brought additional warmth to her cheeks. His smile was approving.

For the first time she noticed the crow's feet at the corners of his eyes, and Elise wondered how old he was. She wondered a lot of things about him. But that was why they were both here, she reminded herself: to ask questions and get answers.

"Wind of any shade is part and parcel of this area's weather," she responded. "Mostly it comes in off the ocean. That's why the fog settles so solidly. Today's is a rare easterly, driving the fog back to sea." She shrugged. "I really don't know what the missionaries were thinking of when they named this place White Wind. Maybe there's no phrase in Spanish for pea soup."

Dylan chuckled. "Well, whatever the reason, it's much too nice a day to spend cooped up inside."

Her gaze fell to her hands as they rested on the door's ledge. It was exactly what she'd been thinking, yet she was reluctant to admit as much to him. She had an inkling he meant to spend the day with her—off her turf and the security it brought with it. Last night she'd had time to think about what had happened between them yesterday, the tacit understanding they'd come to. His suggestion—for he really hadn't ever come out and stated it as fact—that they'd shared a relationship in another time, another place, was ridiculous. Absurd. And yet she had no explanation for how he knew intimate details about her. On reflection, it terrified her. She felt violated, as if a stranger had ransacked her home, pawed through her belongings. She'd begun to wonder what else he knew, what private things he was privy to.

But beyond the threat of not knowing was still the powerful incentive to know.

"Would you like to come in?" Elise asked, hoping to take the initiative.

"Actually, I've chartered a sloop down at the harbor," Dylan said. "I thought you might like to go sailing on the bay."

"Sailing?"

"You love to...I mean, you might like sailing, Elise." His expression remained straightforward, but she saw his jaw tighten at his slip of the tongue that seemed to irritate him. But he'd already told her, that first evening when he cornered her near the gallery, that they'd sailed together. *I taught you, took you out your first time.* "You've never been before?"

It was definitely a question, but she could tell what he wanted the answer to be. No, he didn't want to tell her what they'd been to each other; he wanted her to tell him. Unaccountably, his machinations stung her, even though he'd made no secret that he was here to make her remember.

"I've never been on a sailboat in my life," she said defiantly.

"Well, there's always a first time, right?" His gaze shifted away from her face, and Elise had the impression of strong emotions being held in check. She'd seen it before in him— the constant reining back, that obvious effort not to say more. Or to contradict. "You'll be perfectly safe. I'm an expert sailor. I've got more than enough warm clothes for the both of us. And the boat's rigged so it can be handled by one person, so you won't have to do anything strenuous. I know you're still mending from your accident."

So he, too, was going to treat her like porcelain. "I imagine I could handle myself," she said tartly. She *was* getting better.

"Then you'll go?"

Would she? Elise peered up at him, into his black gaze which strove to be candid and trustworthy, and succeeded, to a degree. Yes, she'd be safe with him—physically. He couldn't completely hide, however, the pain that hovered near the edge of his gaze. The hurt, the frustration and confusion, the fervent wanting that couldn't help but be a threat to her well-being, no matter what.

She could have been looking into her own eyes.

"I need to lock up first, put a note on the door," Elise said. "And I should call my aunt." She turned away from him, reluctant to acknowledge his discernible relief. His vulnerability touched her, too much. It made her want to help him, but that would have left her own spirit exposed.

Elise closed the shutters, checked the latch on the back door, and removed the key from the cash register. Then she dialed her aunt's phone number.

"Aunt Char? It's me," she said. "I wanted to let you know I'm taking the day off, closing up the gallery. It's such a gorgeous day, I thought I'd take advantage of it, get out in the sun. In case Keith needs me..." She watched Dylan watch her from his post just outside the door. *In case he needs me.* "If Keith should call, tell him I've gone off with a friend. I'll be home by dinnertime." She said goodbye and replaced the receiver.

They both simply stood there for a moment, gazes locked. She hadn't lied, Elise told herself. She hadn't. She was going with Dylan because she wanted answers to her questions. This wasn't a romantic liaison, and she had nothing to feel guilty about.

"So you're free, then?" Dylan asked.

She nodded. "Yes. Yes, I am."

The boat was smaller than she'd thought it would be, but it was still equipped with a cabin one entered by descending three narrow steps. There were a tiny stove and oven, and hot and cold running water at the miniature sink. A small table to eat at, and a fairly large bunk for sleeping. It even had a bathroom—an exceedingly cramped one, but a bathroom nonetheless.

Dylan kept up a steady stream of commentary, inundating her with sailing jargon as he explained what he was doing as he set up the boat and got them underway. The charter manager, a grizzled man Elise didn't know personally, watched as Dylan skillfully maneuvered out of the dock, then motored past the other sailboats tucked in their slips. Once he saw they were safely away, the older man waved cheerfully and returned to the charter office.

Elise adjusted the bulky life jacket under which she wore a large sweater she suspected was Dylan's. It certainly smelled like him—a pleasant after-shave mingling with singular maleness. She wouldn't have thought she'd have yet had the opportunity—nor the inclination—to identify his scent. But she *had* pressed her face to his wide chest on two different occasions. In any case, the warm essence of him around her was comforting.

He'd settled her on a seat near him as he manned the wheel. Once they'd cleared the dock, though, he was never in one place for long; she watched in fascination as, again accompanying his actions with explanation, he cut the engine, brought in and stowed the fenders, unfurled the jib and made it fast and hoisted the mainsail. It luffed in the breeze for a few moments until Dylan could return to the helm. He twirled the wheel, eyes narrowed at the pale triangular expanse. Suddenly, the sail caught the breeze and swelled. And they were off.

Her hair whipped out behind her as Elise turned her face into the wind. She gasped against its ice-cap chill, but the sun was equator warm in a delicious contradiction of sensations that brought her skin to life. That brought *her* to life.

Yes, she was free. *This* was what she needed, what, had she known it were an option, she'd have chosen to do today above all other activities. Her spirit lifted and filled much as the mainsail did. The boat sang over the water with a pulse and bound that made their ride even more thrilling. Ignorant as she was, Elise knew Dylan's skill smoothed their course. The boat heeled slightly, and she braced her feet against the deck as she studied him. The wind was creating havoc with his hair, skimming it off his forehead and revealing the strong, perfect bone structure of his face. The wind's bite brought color to his cheeks, replacing the single-toned sepia coloring that had made him seem less dimensional and therefore less real to her. At this moment, though, he'd lost his phantom quality, was no longer the mysterious genie conjured from a hidden past. No, today he was a man, vibrant and real and *now*. He was in control, and it seemed to Elise his own troubles lifted from his shoulders. He was accustomed to being in control. Knowing that he was right now made a few of her burdens lighter. The hazard he presented disappeared as surely as the fog, for she couldn't look at him in this light and feel afraid. At least not in the same way, Elise thought as sudden desire shot up her spine, like mercury in a thermometer that had been abruptly plunged into hot liquid.

How did you know? she wanted to ask him. Dylan was obviously passionate about sailing. And through his obsession he had chosen the perfect activity to banish her ailments, fill her with energy and pique her interest in him so effectively she couldn't not feel closer to him. But of course that was the nature of passion, of feeling passionate about something or someone, as she had—could—about her painting. She'd noticed that quality in Dylan from the very first, for such depth of emotion was inherently fascinating; people wanted to witness it, to believe they had it within them to feel so themselves. The joy, Elise reflected, was that each person did have that ability. The tragedy was that many never experienced it to its fullest simply because intense emotion called for a person to look deeply into oneself and accept what one found. And so many people were afraid of what such self-examination would reveal about their natures. But until a person faced what he feared most, he would never identify what could set him—or her—free.

Dylan glanced down and caught her looking at him. "Are we having fun yet?" he shouted with the quirk of a smile that was just a little bit unsure, and terribly endearing.

"Yes," she answered over the roar of the wind and the gentle hiss of the hull as it knifed through the water. "Makes me wish I could do more things like this."

"Why don't you?"

A lock of hair blew across her eyes and she brushed it back. "Well, I don't exactly fit the description of a starving artist, but I don't have much money for outings or vacations. I'd like to see some places, though, before I... someday. Even though I have a tendency to hole up like a hermit, I think I could get the travel bug real easy."

"Where would you go, Elise, if you could go anywhere in the world?"

She slid him a questioning glance. Was he flirting with her? "Anywhere?"

He tossed an open hand into the air, as if he could grant her her greatest wish. "Anywhere." He *was* flirting with her.

She couldn't help being drawn in by his charm. "Well..." She thought about his question. *Far, far away from Viento Blanco* came the answer, as it had the other night. "Someplace warm." She looked out across the shimmering water. The ocean had a tangible quality to it today. "Along the shore would be nice. But no fog!"

"Got it. No fog."

"Unless, of course, it's wafting over the Seine as it flows through Paris, and I'm watching it from a snug little café while I sip an espresso and rest my aching feet after spending the entire day in the Louvre."

"Ah, yes—Paris. The artists' mecca."

"Unfortunately it's a rather expensive mecca. Oh, well," Elise sighed without rancor.

She watched as Dylan brought the boat closer to the wind. Or at least it seemed closer—whatever that meant. "Ever consider a trip to Mexico?" he asked abruptly. "It's got all your requirements—warm, near the ocean, relatively inexpensive. Gorgeous sunsets, endless beaches . . . ?'' his voice trailed off questioningly.

Elise tipped her chin in puzzlement at his inflection. "Sounds wonderfully romantic. I'll have to remember that option when—" She bit back the rest of her sentence. *When Keith and I finally take a honeymoon.* For some reason she was reluctant to bring Keith's name into the conversation, and she felt a twinge of guilt at that aversion.

Like a solar eclipse, Dylan's expression turned distinctly cold. Aloof. Then she remembered his words: *We took midnight walks on the beach. We did . . . everything together.* But she didn't remember.

Elise searched her mind for a way to breach the gulf that had suddenly sprung up between them. She didn't mean to hurt him, truly she didn't, yet it seemed she could so easily. *You shouldn't expect so much from people,* she almost told him her own self-admonishment.

"Thanks for asking me to come sailing with you today, Dylan," she said. His eyes met hers, evaluating, and she smiled in emphasis of her words. "I mean it. It's just what I needed."

The tension in his features eased. "You're welcome." Something in her own face made him smile back, his pleasure in her pleasure quite apparent. She smiled even wider, even as her breathing stalled. She hadn't seen him look so happy, not since... Again she realized how handsome, how potent a presence he was. It didn't seem that he could be here just for her.

She wanted to sketch him, as he was now. She wanted to touch him as she had before. And she wasn't here to do either. Neither was he.

"You love this," she announced. "Sailing, I mean."

"It's a part of me, like eating or sleeping," he concurred. "I miss it when I don't get to go out regularly."

"Where'd you learn?"

"Chesapeake. I grew up in the southwest, but I graduated from Annapolis. Went out on the bay with a friend that first time and I was hooked."

"It must have been in your blood, then. I mean, sailing never caught on with me, even though I grew up around Boston—" Elise cut herself off as her gaze flew to his in confusion. He knew, of course, where she was from. She'd told him already. Or rather, he'd told her, in so many words.

The strangeness of their circumstances struck her anew. It was unnerving. What did he know about her? That sense of invasion crawled through her again. It wasn't fair that he should know the kinds of things she didn't know about him. Not yet, at least.

"Ready to tack?" he asked, diverting her thoughts.

"Tack?"

"We need to change directions. I'm going to have you take the helm. Then when I give the word, I want you to turn the wheel so you're heading straight for that lighthouse on the horizon. The bow will swing around, and the boat'll heel the other way, so make sure you take a wide stance. Just concentrate on heading for that lighthouse. I'll handle the sheets."

Elise frowned. "Sounds complicated. What if I goof and capsize the boat or something?"

It was the wrong thing to say, she realized immediately. His gaze was pinned to the sails, ever alert, but it changed at her skeptical comment. Hardened. He'd promised her safety. She'd expressed doubt. It struck her that this was Dylan's fear, not having her trust. Perhaps, Elise mused, in this past he talked about, he felt he had done something to erode that trust. *If I'd known you were hurt, I'd have come to you, no matter the distance or circumstances.*

Why had he left in the first place? Or had she left him, and if so, why? What had he done?

You just weren't there.

"You're right," Dylan said tersely. "Maybe you'd be better off below, out of the way."

"I'm not an invalid!" she shouted against the snap of the wind. "I didn't mean I couldn't do it." She gripped the outer railing, more in anger than for leverage, and set her jaw stubbornly. "Just tell me when you want to come about."

Dylan's eyes pierced her like a hawk's, a feral but practiced watchfulness that startled her. Then she realized why he looked at her so. The phrase had slipped from her lips without her thinking. It wasn't that technical a sailing term—"to come about"—but that she'd used it how and when she had was unusual for someone who claimed to know nothing of sailing.

She could have picked up the expression anywhere. Sailing vernacular was part of everyday usage—people talked about maintaining an even keel in their lives, or taking a different tack in solving a problem. She herself used such terms frequently. It was absurd to even entertain the notion that she might possess a latent sailing experience.

Dylan knew it, too, yet he'd chosen this activity today precisely to jar such an experience from her memory. She was almost sorry to see his effort fail. Elise wondered what he'd have done had the weather not cooperated with his plans in so timely a manner. Another picnic basket? But the fact was the weather and everything else had conspired perfectly in an extraordinary moment that could only lend credence to this man's claims.

But you don't want to remember. And you want more than answers. You want a reason that this has happened to you.

Disturbed, Elise glanced away.

Dylan coaxed the boat onto the precise heading he wanted before having her take the wheel. It was cold and hard in her hands, and she grasped it with a determination to perform well. Her concentration was perilously hindered by his proximity as he stood behind her, an arm reaching out from behind her periodically to correct her heading.

It wasn't long before she got the hang of it. Dylan moved forward and loosely held two lines—sheets, he'd called them—in the palms of his gloved hands. The wind puffed, slacking a bit before a stronger gust hit them.

"Ready about?" he asked.

"Ready," Elise answered.

"Hard alee!"

The wheel spun in her hand far more naturally than she would have thought it could, and the bow swung sharply to the left. Elise shifted as the boat did, from port to starboard. Dylan let go of the leeward side jib sheet. He caught up the other sheet, pulled it in on its winch and cleated it, all with a fluid swiftness. The boom swung across, and the sloop heeled the other way. Without a hitch, they had brought her around.

She watched him trim the sheet, hope and discouragement still warring on his face. They gathered speed again.

"Now what?" she asked.

"I thought we'd head for an inlet near here. The charter manager said it would be a nice place to drop anchor and have lunch."

The little cove wasn't far, and within a half hour the boat was bobbing gently in calm waters. Dylan provided the fare again: shrimp-salad sandwiches overflowing with tomato slices and lettuce. Though the food was delicious, there was no apparent significance in his choice today. Or perhaps there was, and this time it failed to stir a connection in her. She refused to ask.

He sat across from her, his long legs stretched out, his casually crossed ankles inches from her demurely crossed ones. As the sun warmed them, they abandoned their thick outerwear. Elise couldn't help noticing how Dylan's loose-fitting sweater still managed to cling to all the right places on his arms and torso. They ate without speaking, the tension between them still taut. And he watched her. Even in silence, it seemed he wanted something from her; even in silence, she resisted giving him anything.

The activity, wind and sun stimulated Elise's determination. It was time, she decided, to get what *she* wanted: explanations. Logical ones.

"Tell me, Dylan Colman—what do you do when you're not traveling through time in search of old acquaintances?" At his reproachful look, she leaned forward from the waist and confided, "I'm joking." And she was—almost.

He frowned at the half-eaten sandwich in his hand. "I never said I traveled through time."

"No, and you never exactly said we've known each other in another incarnation. You've done some pretty strong suggesting, though."

"If I have suggested things, it's because the truth hurts, to use an old saying. At least my truth seems to hurt you. Each time I've tried to tell you about us, it's nearly killed you." He raised his eyes to hers. "And I don't want to hurt you, Elise, no matter what...crisis either of us is facing. I'd almost rather leave again than cause you that kind of pain."

His concern touched her anew even while his implication that he might leave—*again?*—roused an instant fear in her, like furies awakening from the slumber of a hundred years. Would he go before she had a chance to discover if he held the key to her recovery? "I haven't felt a twinge all morning," she said.

"Of either pain or remembrance, right?" He straightened and flung the remains of his sandwich skyward. A circling gull, one of scores that wheeled and keened in the air surrounding the boat, swooped down to snatch the crust seconds before it would have hit the water and become fair game for his cronies. "I can't tell what you know or might know, and what you don't remember. Or can't."

"Then we're in the same boat." His eyes cut to hers and she smiled. "To use an old saying. I don't know what you know about me and it's damned disconcerting." She lifted one shoulder. "Perhaps if we set aside remembering for a while. Don't talk about us. Just tell me about...you."

He thought this over. "Will you let me know if your head starts to hurt?" he asked.

If she'd learned nothing else over the past two days, she'd learned she had to press on, despite the pain. "Let me worry about my own head."

"I mean it, Elise. I refuse to put either of us through another experience like yesterday. Promise you'll stop me at the first sign of pain, or I'll hoist the anchor right now and take this boat back to Viento Blanco."

Elise met his eyes with defiance. His gaze never gave an inch. And she was suddenly glad. Glad that he put her welfare above his most pressing need to make her remember. She realized that, despite his discouragement, she *had* begun to trust him in the past twenty-four hours, and his actions now extended that trust just a little bit more.

She began to see how she might have loved this man, once upon a time.

"All right," she said, unable to prevent a dry smile. "You do drive a hard bargain, Mr. Colman."

"It's my job," he answered.

It was an apt transition. "What is?"

"Mmm. You would pick that subject." He pressed the pads of three fingers to each eye and gave a short, rueful laugh. "I don't know if I should tell you, after your quick deduction the other day about how I knew things about you." He took a deep breath as his hands fell away from his face and he looked at her. "I'm a negotiator. For the government."

"The government? You mean, like, the United States government?"

"Yes. I'm afraid I can't give you many details about what I do. I've been out of the country for several months now, working on a six-man team moderating some very...volatile relations between us and...other countries." He grimaced. "I know I sound incredibly vague, but I have no choice. It's a matter of national security. It must seem as if, because I can't talk about certain things, I'm hiding something. And after the way most of my revelations have affected you, the implication is that what I'm hiding is bad. It's not, really—I do a lot of good in my work. But it's not the kind of job where a man can come home from the office and tell his wife about the successes he had at work that day.''

He paused, locking his gaze with hers, as if he wanted her to understand very clearly what he said next. ''Believe me, I'm being as frank as I can with you, Elise. I've always been as honest with you as I could be.''

His words did indeed sink in. Sympathy for the difficult position he was in rose in her—to possess such vital information that one had to constantly evaluate: what to tell, what to hold back. What to give in on, on what to stand fast. She couldn't imagine what it would be like to be entrusted with mediating a situation that could affect the future of millions of lives.

And that dilemma directly paralleled their own circumstances. What could he tell her? What information about them would she respond to and what would she reject? It helped, she realized, to know more about him, to know what moved him, drove him, made his life worth living. Strangely, though knowing more about Dylan Colman made him more tangible, he became even more mysterious.

''It sounds like quite a responsibility,'' she said. ''I can't even imagine the skills one would need to do a job like that.''

He leaned forward, elbows on his knees, his clasped hands between them. The movement brought him closer to her. ''A strong knowledge of military strategy, for one.''

''From Annapolis,'' she surmised. He'd told her.

''Yes.''

''What made you decide to go there, instead of a southwestern college closer to where you grew up?''

''I wanted to do something that contributed directly to society. Serving my country seemed the best way.'' He rubbed his thumb, back and forth, over the back of his other one as he talked. ''I don't have a creative gift, like you, Elise. I didn't have a calling, the kind that can't be denied. But I did feel . . . something that compelled me.''

Elise avoided his eyes, as if her gaze would reveal that denying her gift had been exactly what she'd been doing for months. "You sound as if you feel a need to justify yourself."

"Not at all. I simply think it's important you know why I do what I do, even if I can't tell you exactly what that is. I'd rather try to relate to you in that aspect of my job because I believe you feel the same way about your art. What we do says a lot about who we are."

"I see." She had to agree with him. Her work was more than an occupation; it fulfilled her deeply. And she'd lost it.

No, wait...perhaps she'd lost only the outlet of such emotions—not the ability to feel itself. Maybe she needed to let her art go and search for another vocation that would bring meaning to her life. Could it be that her resistance at accepting such a fate was what had been tearing her in two?

But never again to express herself through her art, never paint again!

"You might have a point," she allowed herself to admit. "I've always believed that fulfillment can come from almost any source—" Elise gave him a wry smile "—and not necessarily creative. A person can make an art out of whatever they do." She hesitated, searching for an example. "My father was that way. He was an electrician, believe it or not. Can you get any more prosaic? But he enjoyed people. He liked helping them. My mother was quieter but had the same knack. She used to go out on calls with him and chat with his customers while he worked."

"You mean before your parents died," Dylan said with sympathy.

Elise felt her features go slack with shock. "You know about my parents?" *How* did he know?

"You'd mentioned once that you were an only child, that you had a great-aunt in California, your only living relative. I assumed...though you didn't seem inclined to talk about it, it hadn't seemed a painful subject. I guess I thought they'd died when you were pretty young and your aunt had raised you." He studied her. "I take it by your re-action that's not so?"

"My mother and father were killed, Dylan."

Shock now jolted his features. "Your parents were *killed?*"

Elise regarded him. "So. There are a few things about me you don't know." For some reason, she wasn't gratified by this discovery, because now she wanted him to know, if only so she wouldn't have to explain.

"I never... I mean, obviously you never told me."

She squinted out across the water. "I guess I don't talk about my parents much—in this life or any other."

Neither of them spoke for several minutes. When Dylan did, his voice carried the muted quality it'd had when he'd questioned her about her accident. "I'm... so sorry, Elise. What... when did it happen? I want to know, if you'd like to tell me," he said softly. He seemed to have overcome his initial shock. Instead, his face wore that dispassionate cast she'd now come to realize signified anything but detach-ment. "If it's too painful, though—"

"No," Elise said. She didn't feel pain anymore when she thought about her parents' deaths. Just a... a numbness she'd long ago decided must be acceptance. "There was a storm one night. My father got a call. A customer in the country had a sump pump in his cellar short out, blowing a fuse. My father said he'd go on over and take a look. My mother went with him."

"Were they... were they electrocuted?"

"No. On the road out to this house there's a narrow bridge at the bottom of a hill. That night, the river had swelled and swamped the road. My parents never saw the car stalled on the bridge until it was too late..."

Elise swallowed against the tightness in her throat. Per-haps she wasn't as numb as she'd believed.

"My God, Ellie, how old were you?"

"Seventeen." She concentrated on the roughened texture of the boat's seat against one palm, on the hue and cry of the sea gulls. She squinted harder at the rugged coastline, as if she expected to find adequate distraction from her thoughts. "That's when I came to live with Aunt Charlotte."

Out of the corner of her eye, she saw Dylan extend his hand toward her, almost touching her, but something stopped him mid-gesture. "I can't imagine how you bore such a loss."

"I don't know either." She noticed that her voice held a certain detachment as well. "I remember, all I could think about was that it seemed so...senseless. The flooding hadn't been life threatening. No one was going to die if the pump wasn't fixed immediately. And my mother didn't have to go with my father that night. But she did. Duty called—called them both. It was better that way. I don't think either one of them would have wanted to live without the other."

"But I don't think either one of them would have wanted you to be so alone."

Elise said nothing, thinking about his last comment. Then she turned and found his gaze on her, as intent as if he were trying to see through her. "You must have been very hurt," he said. "Very...angry."

"Oh, I hurt—" Unexpectedly, a searing longing went through her, surprising Elise out of her impassivity and nearly overwhelming her. *When did it stop?* she wondered. Did everyone carry a flickering hope in the deepest corner of their hearts that the impossible would happen and their loved ones would come back to them? Surely, after seven long years, she shouldn't be feeling this way.

She cleared her throat and went on, hoping that Dylan hadn't noticed her lapse, "—but was I angry? What would have been the point? My parents were dead. I couldn't be mad at them. Yes, I was angry that they'd gone out for such a trivial reason. But after a while I told myself that both of them had only been doing what they wanted to do...."

Elise dropped her chin and noticed that she still held the rest of her sandwich in stiffened fingers, and she realized how long she'd been talking. How much she had revealed. How much she could remember, vividly, of that period in her life. Why, if she had to forget something, couldn't it have been that?

"I apologize for running on," she said stiffly. "We were going to talk about you."

"Elise. Don't clam up on me now."

She said nothing, still staring at her sandwich and trying vainly to figure out and control, all at once, the torrential emotion coursing through her.

Dylan made a small sound of exasperation. "All right then, I'll talk. I think that you are very brave, Elise Nash."

She shook her head vehemently. "No." If only he knew.

"Yes, brave—to survive your parents' deaths, and now to be struggling back to health from your own near-death experience. You have such a quiet strength, a dependability," Dylan went on, his voice musing. "I think it's that quality that drew me to you, what made me believe you'd be there when I came back—"

He broke off, frustration overtaking his features like a cloud covering the sun. Even if it weren't so apparent, she still would have known he waged a constant battle not to say more to her, or too much.

With a suddenness, Elise wanted him to say whatever it was he felt he couldn't—because she wanted to believe in something again. She wanted that hope of a man being able to forge an incredible link and regain that which was impossible to regain: the past. Yesterday he'd suggested he had done as much, but now she needed to know the truth.

Because if it really were possible, then she might have a chance.

Chapter Five

She couldn't look at him, wouldn't let him see what she was asking of him. "You have certain qualities, too, Dylan," Elise said in a low voice. "A presence that's compelling, almost... irresistible. I think you could make me believe that nearly anything was possible."

He lifted her chin with one finger. She had no choice but to meet his gaze. "Can I?" he asked.

"You must know the kind of power you have," she whispered, closing her eyes against the river of yearning rising up in her at his touch. God help her, she did want to feel again. To believe. "I don't need to know exactly what you do as a negotiator to venture that you're very, very good at it."

"It mostly takes a good insight into human nature." His breath fanned across her cheek. "You need to figure out why people do what they do."

Elise opened her eyes. "That's what you're doing with me, isn't it?" she asked. "Trying to figure out why I don't remember you."

His face was scant inches from hers. His black eyes searched hers. "Yes," he answered softly, "though there's something else I want even more."

No, he wouldn't say it, but his implication was crystal clear. *Oh, God.* She stared at him, stricken by her mistake—in coming here, in being with him today, in asking of him the reassurance she wanted. Because she had her answer: he loved her. He'd already told her so. And what he wanted, what he needed, was for her to love him. This was the link; this was what *he* wanted to recapture.

Wasn't that what you wanted to know?

She tried to withdraw from his touch but stopped because she couldn't escape the dominion of his eyes, depthless as pooled midnight. She could almost see herself in them. *The mirrors of the soul.* Abruptly, Elise found herself looking at the situation from his side: what if she loved him deeply? What if she wanted him as profoundly as she knew without a doubt that he wanted her—she heard it in his voice, saw it in his face, beheld it in his kiss. What would it be like to contain an unending tide of emotion, because the person she loved didn't know her, trust her, believe her—or love her?

The aspects of her own struggle rose up and obliterated any other perspective. *I don't know him!* But did she truly want to know and trust and believe in this man? God knew she wanted to respond to the appeal in his gaze—wondered at times how she'd be able to resist—but did she want to love him?

Was it what he asked of her that frightened her, or the way he wanted it? He believed she could love without reserve, but she couldn't. No, she couldn't. Not anymore.

Or not yet?

"You think there's a reason, too, that I don't remember. Don't you, Dylan?" She reached out, clutched shoulders that were like rock beneath her palms. "Before I can love...before anything else, I need to know first why I don't remember you. I haven't been able to paint since my accident," she confessed, almost in shame. But she had to make him understand what *she* wanted, more than anything. "It's like . . . there's nothing here," she pressed the tip of her index finger to her temple, "nothing to use. It's gone, whatever it was that inspired me. I've never before experienced one second when my hands didn't literally itch for a brush or a pencil or charcoal. My art was always . . . like your sailing. Like breathing."

Tears filled her eyes. "I need that expression of myself, Dylan. Part of me is missing without it. Some days I long for it so much and I'm so afraid . . . oh, God, I'm so afraid I'll never have it back!"

Abruptly, Dylan stood and pulled her into his arms. "It'll come back to you, Ellie," he assured her as she struggled to find her own center without giving in to the refuge in his strength. "You can't stop believing it will."

"Believing!" she choked. "Believing or wanting with every cell of me doesn't work! Just like wanting to remember you won't make me remember! I've got to find a reason why I can't paint anymore, but—" she choked again "—*what if there is no reason?*"

She had never voiced this, her greatest terror, to anyone. No, she'd tried with all her might to block it from her mind as she attempted, much as Dylan counseled, to believe that with her gradual recovery, her talent would come back to her. But it hadn't. It hadn't! And she'd grown so weary of waiting.

Dylan pulled her closer, his empathy palpable as Elise lost her battle for composure and at last sobbed out her frustration, mourned her loss. Regret racked her, but sheer fury fought the battle against it. *What have I done to deserve this fate?* The inequity of it raised an army bent on reprisal, even while the release from this terrible secret cleansed her as one shriven. And it was because, like yesterday at the gallery, she found understanding and solace in Dylan's embrace. She couldn't resist it, didn't want to. Like the cove that protected their small boat, she'd found safe harbor. For now.

Eventually, the tempest spent, she pulled away from him, wiping away tears with the backs of her hands. The wind, the sun and now the wetness had chapped her skin. Dylan brushed away her fingers, cupping her face in his palms and soothing away the sting with the feather-light grazing of his thumbs.

"I—I'm sorry," she stammered, losing more and more of her cognizance with every stroke of his thumbs. She'd emptied herself of so much emotion she was utterly defenseless to this man's appeal. "I don't usually break down like that." She glanced up at him. "Do I?"

One corner of his mouth tipped up as he shook his head, *no, you don't* and *no apology necessary* at the same time. His gaze roved over her features, caressing them, as his fingers brushed back her unruly hair.

He couldn't think her brave now. Not after this. Her cheeks heated up and stung afresh. "I must look a sight," she said as an excuse to draw away from him. She reached up to pull her thick mane into some kind of order.

"Don't, Ellie." He caught her hands and guided them back to their former place, palms resting against his chest. Then he plunged his own hands into her hair. "You really don't know how beautiful you are to me, do you?" Tenderness suffused his features, bathing her in a glow. "Give me one minute, please, to stand here and look at you. I haven't had the chance to savor seeing you again, just being with you again. Especially like this, with the sunshine in your hair. You belong in the sun, you know, with your golden hair and golden eyes. It's how I always pictured you, all those days and nights...." He bit down on the rest of his sentence, his jaw bulging with his restraint, then seemed to decide to go on despite it. "No, Elise, I'm no artist like you, with your sense of composition, but I see you in bright colors that go with the gold—like red. I see you in red."

"Red? I don't think so.... It isn't me."

"It is, Elise. It's more you than any other color on earth."

"Is that why you dress in black, then?" she accused lightly, trying still to find a little distance, "because *it's* you?"

"Do you have another suggestion?"

She stared up at him, close enough now to discern for the first time the subtle difference in shading between the iris and pupil of his eyes. The irises weren't black but a deep smoky gray striated with black, making them look like the shutter of a camera. His pupils, however, were pure shadow, their aperture wide open and dilated even in the near blinding sunlight.

"I've never known anyone with eyes quite like yours," she murmured.

"But you have, Elise. Believe me, you have."

Yes, black belonged to him—completely absorbing of light and its many tricks and layers, taking everything in. Making the world his own. Making her world his.

It was just a way of phrasing the words, but Elise realized that Dylan actually "saw" her in red—had seen her so before, or believed he had. And at that moment, she found she could believe, too.

Almost of their own volition, her hands rose and threaded through his coal black wind-tossed hair. To hold him fast. To hold him here.

"Ellie." His fingers clenched in her own hair. "God knows how much I want to kiss you right now. So badly. But I don't want to hurt you."

Control . . . he wanted control, desperately, but she could tell he was on the verge of losing it. The skin across his cheekbones was stretched taut. His brows slashed downward over his eyes; his mouth was a rigid line. There was nothing handsome about a man under such strain, Elise thought. But nothing was more real and honest than the raw emotion sketched on his face. Real and absolute and *now*.

"You won't hurt me," she whispered.

"I have in the past—"

"You won't," she said again, and pulled his head down to find his lips with hers.

With that contact his hesitation disappeared and he took her lips hungrily, opening them with a delicious pressure, consuming them with his warm, wet, soft mouth. Thumbs against her temples, fingers cradling the back of her head, he angled her chin upward and found deeper access to her mouth. The stroke of his tongue across hers was met with a soft moan from Elise, a low groan from Dylan. His arms went around her, a cocoon of steel, and from knee to collarbone their bodies clung to each other, sealing their bond.

And belonging settled in Elise like a much used, well-loved brush would fit into her hand.

His mouth left hers and roved across her cheek to find her earlobe, catching it between his lips as he mumbled something around it.

Elise fought for coherence. "What?"

"Your head," he murmured, so close to her ear it was as if he'd entered her brain. "Has it begun to hurt at all?"

She would have sworn a lie on her parents' graves if she'd had to. She didn't. "No."

"Good. Because I think it would kill me to stop touching you right now," Dylan said as his mouth melded to hers again on his sharp inhalation, the gentle suction tugging at her and fixing her even more securely in his embrace.

No, there was no pain. On the contrary, the cobwebby feeling in her head, which had never completely abated since her accident, decreased—as if the wind that had swept the fog away whistled through her brain, cleaning all the musty corners of her mind. She felt gloriously alive for the first time in months. The joy and wonder of it leapt up in her, a cripple throwing down crutches and standing alone. The day became brighter, the breeze sweeter and her heart a little lighter. *Because this is right.* They had found and completed the connection that had hung so tenuously between them the first time he'd kissed her.

"Dylan. I need to know," she said against his mouth. "Tell me, truly, what *you* believe. Do you believe this is destiny or fate or whatever? Were we...are we soul mates?"

Dylan raised his head and stared into her eyes. He didn't have to tell her, for she could see what he believed—and what he wanted. And Elise discovered that there was one question she wasn't ready to have answered:

Were we...lovers?

His eyes met her inquiry, and Elise felt suddenly cheated, as she had felt cheated of her life these past four months. To have loved this man so thoroughly and not know it! But she didn't want to know—because if they had, and she couldn't remember, she instinctively knew the reason must be as powerful as the love they'd shared.

Why had he left in the first place? The questions that had leapt to mind earlier now echoed in her brain. *Had she left him, and if so why? What had he done?*

Elise pulled away from him slowly, her mind a whirlwind of confusion and sudden doubt. And fear.

He reached for her. "Elise—"

"I think we should go back."

His gaze narrowed before his eyelids flickered in discouragement. In disappointment, as if she had failed him— again. And damn her traitorous heart, she couldn't help feeling a vestige of guilt, a profusion of regret.

"Yes," he said, "the wind's changed. It looks like the fog's coming in."

She peered out to sea. Sure enough, far in the distance, a hazy white ridge, like a gigantic snowbank, sat on the horizon. "It certainly looks ominous," she observed with a sudden shiver, hating the thought of being under that shroud again.

Dylan had already begun stowing away the remains of their lunch. "A sailor's worst nightmare is fog—navigation by sight is shot to hell, hazards are hidden just as surely as the safe way home. Any sailor worth his salt makes a run for his mooring at the first sign of a fog bank."

"Are we in danger?" she asked.

"Once we're back out in the open, the wind'll be behind us. We'll make good time." He glanced up and caught her expression. "I'll get you home safely, Elise. You can trust me that far, at least."

But she wasn't afraid so much as depressed by the incoming fog. It meant their moment in the sun was coming to an end.

Within minutes they had raised the sails and were on their way. Elise found she couldn't keep her eyes away from the clearly defined billow on the horizon. It seemed like a giant wave or an avalanche, and it was coming toward them with startling swiftness. By nightfall Viento Blanco would be covered by it, much as she imagined Brigadoon disappeared into the mist for its century-long hibernation.

Maybe *she* was the one out of step, out of time—not Dylan.

Some of her thoughts must have shown on her face, for she felt a hand on her shoulder in reassurance. "Don't worry," he said. "We've got plenty of time." But it didn't seem to her that they did.

"Maybe this is the missionaries' *viento blanco*," she mused aloud. "I'd always thought, or imagined actually, that the white wind this place was named for was good. A sign of faith or hope or something that the missionaries witnessed. Not this grim wall of gloom." For some reason, part of her instruction in art came back to her at that moment: in pigments, she recalled, the merging of all colors was black; yet in light, all color merged into white.

What had the sun revealed today? Did the camouflaging fog follow Dylan—or her? Did she truly want to know the truth about Dylan Colman... the truth about herself?

It seemed, Elise reflected, that rather than getting answers today, she had only raised more questions.

Dylan stopped the car at a corner two blocks from the gallery. He killed the ignition and turned to study the woman who'd been silent since they'd docked the sloop. He could guess what troubled her.

"Elise."

Golden eyes met his. She'd gotten some color today and it made her skin even more incandescent, if that were possible. Her lips were still rosy and swollen. Was it just him, or would it be obvious to the person on the street that she'd been thoroughly kissed this afternoon? A certain sense of male satisfaction left him gratified he'd placed his mark upon her. On the other hand, he was a marked man himself.

"I want to see you again tomorrow," he said.

"I can't. I've got a doctor's appointment in San Francisco."

"I'll take you, then."

"No," she said, shaking her head emphatically. Almost in fear.

"Why, Elise?" he asked as gently as he could.

"Because...Keith's taking me."

He'd guessed right. "You could tell him you've decided to drive yourself," Dylan suggested.

"No." Elise averted her face, but not before he caught the look on her face. It *was* fear. Of Hurston? What kind of hold did that bastard have over her?

Almost immediately, Dylan recognized the irrationality of such thoughts and what they revealed about his own state of mind. He'd love to find an excuse, any excuse, to damn the consequences and spirit Elise away from here. With effort he schooled his features, and managed for the hundredth time not to push her. "Then when can I see you again?"

She looked at him, an appeal. "It's not right, Dylan. Seeing each other like this. I'm going to be mar—"

"It *is* right," he interrupted, then once again yanked the choke chain on his impulse to contradict her. "After today, being together in the sun.... Elise, don't you see it's everything else that's wrong? Your head didn't hurt at all the entire afternoon—doesn't that signify something?"

She closed her eyes. "Maybe," she murmured. "But I still need time, Dylan. To think."

They didn't have time! And he was greatly afraid that if she did think about their situation, she'd find an explanation for the feelings that coursed so strongly between them when they were together, and then she'd invent some argument as to why they shouldn't continue to meet. "If not tomorrow, then the next day?" he asked. He couldn't let her go without knowing when he'd see her again—without making her commit to seeing him again. He needed to know she wanted to, even with all her reservations.

"I don't know," Elise said. So she wouldn't promise. It would seem calculated, Dylan realized. Going behind Hurston's back. A betrayal, and Elise Nash was more forthright than that.

That didn't stop you from leaving me, though, did it?

She opened the door to go. "Goodbye, Dylan."

He grabbed her hand and their eyes met. "All right," he said softly. "You go on. But when you do think about it, try not to regret what happened today, Ellie. Please. We did nothing wrong. Don't feel ashamed."

"I . . . I don't." And that was the problem, Dylan concluded as he watched her go.

He sat unmoving as the fog enveloped his car. How he dreaded the thought of a whole day slipping away without seeing her, especially a day when she'd be in Hurston's company the entire time. Hurston was bound to notice the slight sunburn across her cheeks and ask her about it. And what would Elise say? It obviously bothered her to deceive Hurston. Hell, it bothered him, too. But given the choice between complete honesty and losing Elise . . . Dylan already knew the answer to that one.

He half hoped she'd tell Hurston about the two of them. If she had doubts about her relationship with him, it could mean she'd call off the wedding. Hurston himself might call it off. But if she did tell him, Hurston would make good on his claim to run him out of town. *I'd like to see him try.* Regardless, telling Hurston anything about the two of them would jeopardize any chance of seeing her again. And Dylan needed every opportunity he could get to continue convincing her of their love for each other.

Had he made any progress on that front today, or had he done more damage? He couldn't tell. Dylan gripped the steering wheel in suppressed emotion. It was a constant frustration to him, confounding at times, to look up and see plainly how he was a stranger to her, because he expected her to know him and found it incredibly hard to remember she didn't. He had to fight to keep those expectations from defeating him before he even got started with her, for there had been more than one time he'd wanted to say to hell with discretion, take her in his arms, and show her how much he loved her.

And when he finally had…God, the feel of her! How he'd missed her, missed holding her. Missed having the right to. But he had no right to her now. He'd done something to hurt her deeply and it was part of what kept her from remembering. If only he knew what that something was! It had to be some word or deed or action that he wouldn't have considered wrong, because he couldn't have purposely harmed Elise if his life depended on it.

But what if *her* life depended on it? What if, in her perception, the only way she could go on was to block whatever pain or hurt from her mind? She was a strong woman—stubborn and independent. A survivor. She'd have found a way to cope, no matter what, just as she'd coped with her parents' deaths. He was still amazed she'd come out of that experience emotionally intact.

Or maybe she hadn't. Maybe it wasn't what *he'd* done to her, but what someone else had. At first he'd been hurt she hadn't confided in him before about the circumstances of her parents' deaths, yet obviously she seldom talked about it to anyone. He'd known they'd parted that first time because of her doubts, which he'd always believed were about him. But what if they weren't? What if her doubts were about someone else—or herself?

His palm thumped the steering wheel. "That's it!" Then his fingers curled around the leather. Or was he fooling himself? No. In his heart, Dylan knew he'd stumbled on the right answer. Or at least the beginning of an answer to this bizarre predicament. Suddenly he was glad for the time Elise had begged for, because he had some thinking to do as well.

Elise sat at the small secretary in her bedroom and stared out the window into the nothingness of darkness and fog combined. She'd eaten an early dinner with Charlotte and feigned weariness to her aunt, and over the phone to Keith, rather than be in their company this evening. She needed to think. About Dylan.

No, she felt no shame for the afternoon spent with him. But in the hours since then guilt had grown ripe and rotted within her breast, making her seek justification. It hadn't started out as a romantic rendezvous, at least not on her part. She had only wanted to discover what Dylan Colman knew. And she'd certainly discovered a few things—more than she wanted to know, in fact, about either of them.

He wanted her to love him, and she was beginning to—when she already loved another man.

She couldn't be falling in love with Dylan. Elise knew she was not that kind of woman. Her love and loyalty could have only one home at a time. And she loved Keith Hurston.

Yet she could think of nothing but Dylan: his smile, his face, his kiss and how alive she'd felt in his arms. His pull was seductive, the promise in his eyes fascinating and compelling as they told her of what had been—and what had yet to be.

But at this moment all she knew it for was just a promise. Or a memory.

Her gaze fell to the sheet of paper lying on the desk in front of her, a circular she'd found rolled up and stuffed into the handle of her aunt's front door: *Tired of mildew overrunning your life?* How had they guessed? She'd been doodling on the back of it as she sat in thought, words rather than pictures: *FOG* in emphatic, impatient letters, with a box around it; *sail* and *sloop* blew across the page. Suddenly she found herself sketching an eye, then another to match it, both deep set and fringed in masculine lashes, the expression in them . . . intense. Focused. Those eyes begged for a fine straight nose between them, dark, well-defined brows above. The hair was dark also, and windswept above a wide, intelligent forehead. And the jawline . . . ah, nothing would do but strong sure strokes from her pencil. But for the mouth—

Elise's hand froze. She realized she'd been sketching furiously, as if the image poured out of her and she had to capture it like so many raindrops. Each stroke had drawn itself; she merely traced the image. And she had captured it, captured him: Dylan looked back at her, rendered as accurately as any photograph—but for the mouth.

She gripped the pencil harder, as if by doing so she'd master her hesitation. The mouth should be turned up in laughter as it had been today, or at least smiling. Or perhaps curved sensually, irresistibly. It would definitely go with the eyes . . .

Elise could depict none of these alternatives. Whatever motivation that drove her to render the first picture she'd even begun in over four months had deserted her. No! She bent over the page, squeezed her forehead between fingers and thumb and concentrated. Why couldn't she complete Dylan?

Color me blue. The phrase, a line from an old song, popped into her head. But she refused to portray Dylan sad or unhappy or lonely—not by her hand. She couldn't do it! She saw him laughing and in love—just as he saw her in red, wherever and whenever that time once was.

Both of them were in limbo, wishing and waiting and wanting.

Abruptly, the pencil snapped in two in her hand.

Elise stared at it. What she needed was a charcoal pencil and real sketch pad. Painting and drawing weren't only visual arts; there was a texture in the creating of it: the feel of paint smoothing over the canvas, in contrast to the charcoal's rough path, that set a rhythm, a flow. Perhaps if she started over from scratch using the proper tool, she'd be able to finish the portrait of Dylan.

She had the proper tools—in the attic.

Elise nearly upended her chair in her haste to make it to the door of her bedroom, almost as if she must hurry or the impulse would disappear. It was remarkable, really, that she'd drawn anything at all. The realization struck her, bringing quick tears to her eyes. It was a start! And it was because of Dylan.

Elise gave a shaky laugh, sheer relief, as she opened her door and strode to the end of the hallway. Though the light was meager, the attic door's knob was white porcelain and shone bright as a beacon. She grasped it and turned.

And stopped dead.

It was like a wall had gone up, one of brick and barbed wire and dire warnings. That ungodly conflict she'd experienced the very first time she'd seen Dylan Colman lunged out at her.

"No!" Elise cried, gripping the knob tighter. She flattened her palm against the doorjamb for leverage, ready to pull with all her might—as if some force on the other side of the door opposed her.

But it was no outside force that kept her from opening that door. Elise stood for long minutes, contending with her fear: What if there's nothing there?

There was! She had proof!

But what if she opened the sketch pad, took the charcoal between her fingers, and could not give of herself to complete Dylan? In a lightning bolt of insight, Elise knew that what lay beyond that door was a truth she'd rather die than face. A truth she literally couldn't live with.

Slowly, her fingers loosened. Her arm dropped to her side, and Elise laid her forehead against the wooden door in defeat.

Coward. *Coward!*

Self-disgust rose in the back of her throat like bile. She *hated* what she'd become—hesitant and inconstant, unable to face her phobias. Yet she would continue being that way so long as she could rely upon the kindness and strength of others to shore up her own weaknesses in health and character. It wasn't fair to disrupt her aunt's life; it wasn't fair to take advantage of Keith's devotion to her by letting him give her a job, chauffeur her around. Marry her.

And it certainly wasn't right to expect Dylan to have the answers to all her problems.

Patient! Heal *thyself!*

And the truth shall make you free.

Elise straightened. She could conquer at least one fear tonight, by God.

With silent steps she made her way back up the hall and down the stairs. From the darkened kitchen, she could hear muted canned laughter from the television in the parlor, where Aunt Charlotte was. Elise slipped into her coat and reached for the keys, hanging on a peg, to her aunt's ancient Pontiac. She palmed their jangle and crept out the back door.

The carport was not attached to the house but sat fifty feet into the shadowed yard. A stone path had been laid from the back steps to the carport, and Elise picked her way across the yard. Though the car was at least twenty years old, it was still in near mint condition. Aunt Charlotte was the original little old lady who drove only on Sundays. Elise unlocked the door and slid behind the steering wheel.

The interior even smelled new, she thought as she gave herself a moment to steady her breathing. Her heart raced as well, likely more from the stealthiness of her mission than from actual apprehension. She hoped.

The minutes ticked past, and Elise found her breathing and heart rate did indeed return to normal. It was quiet in the car, peaceful. Wisps of fog drifted eerily past the windshield like a mood-setting effect in a teenage fright film. The thought made her smile. Finally, she raised her hand and slid the key into the ignition. With a flick of her wrist she started the car. The engine roared to life, then settled down to a low purr. She turned on the headlights and they made two reassuring circles of light against the front wall of the carport.

Hands shaking, Elise seized the gearshift and put the car into Reverse. It inched out from under the carport and down the paved drive. A surge of triumph went through her as she successfully negotiated the turn onto the street. The fog was as thick as she'd ever seen it, but Elise couldn't let that stop her. She'd be forever waiting for it to evaporate. She

grabbed the gearshift again and slid it two notches down.
Drive.

Then it hit her from the side. Like the blow from a blunt
object, the pain knocked her forward and to the left. The
horn blasted, and she jerked back without thinking. Wrong
move. The back of her head collided with the headrest and
the right side of her skull exploded in agony. Elise gasped.
In a haze, she realized she hadn't actually been struck; she
almost wished she had. Her body had betrayed her again.

Elise made an effort to subdue the pain. *Anger helps,* she
remembered. And fury did indeed fill her at the injustice of
it all. *I don't deserve this kind of pain!* Gritting her teeth,
she concentrated on the nearly inconsequential patch of
road illuminated by the headlights. Damn this fog! Her heel
ground into the floor mat as, fighting back nausea and dizziness, she lifted her foot from the brake pedal and shifted
it to the accelerator.

What are you doing? You could kill yourself!
You shouldn't even be out on a night like this!

"No," Elise moaned. "Oh, please, no." Defeated, she
eased the gearshift back to Park before sagging against the
car door as the vise grip clamping her head between its jaws
tightened with one more tortuous twist.

The door sprang open, nearly spilling her into the street.
"Elise!"

She peered upward through her pain and beheld, by the
dully glowing dome light, her aunt bravely brandishing a
fireplace poker in one hand. Her face was stark white.

A bubble of mirth rose to Elise's lips. Perhaps Charlotte
Nash had some starch in her after all. Then the laughter became a sob. Elise's shoulders slumped and she covered her
face with her hands. "Oh, Aunt Char!"

"What's happened, child?"

"Why can't I . . . drive a car? Something so simple, and I
can't do it!" Her head pulsed, the pressure at its peak.

"But you don't need to drive . . . Keith will take you anywhere you want to go."

"No, he won't," Elise muttered into her hands. "He won't."

"Maybe I should call him—"

"No!" It was the last thing she wanted.

She felt her aunt's puzzlement as Charlotte patted her shoulder, and Elise made an effort to get a grip on herself. But she so wished for tender arms about her at that moment. Mother's arms. Or hard arms, like her father's. Like Dylan's. His empathy and understanding had been a gift, she now realized. And she missed them already.

"Did you two have a disagreement?" Aunt Charlotte asked. "Is that why he didn't come over tonight?" Her voice quavered perilously and Elise flinched.

Just when she thought she'd truly reached the end of her rope, from somewhere within her Elise found the mettle that enabled her to push back the pain and calm herself so that she could calm Aunt Charlotte. "No." She lifted her head, blinking away the tears that watered her eyes. Twice today she'd broken down and cried. It certainly didn't bode well for her recovery.

"It's not…it wasn't that…stranger again, was it?"

"No," Elise said again, this time immeasurably weary. She glanced up and caught her aunt's expression of alarm and doubt. "I'm *fine*. Everything's fine," she said. The pain was receding, leaving her feeling shaky and empty. However, she had no wish to encourage its return. "Could you drive the car back, though?" she asked, and believed her defeat complete.

"Of course, dear," Charlotte said. Elise got out of the car, and the look on her aunt's face tore a fresh patch of guilt through her heart. Her arms went around her aunt in reassurance, giving Charlotte the comfort Elise so wanted for herself. Her relief apparent, Charlotte hugged her back.

It was like being encased in a down pillow, Elise thought, all soft sides that yielded where one wanted them to be firm, as Dylan's embrace had been. The thought brought new tears of longing to her eyes.

But she couldn't depend on Dylan, couldn't allow herself to do so. She had no right to want him or need him, particularly not as she was right now, weak with fear, powerless in the face of her phobias—and especially vulnerable to him. It occurred to her that she had no idea where in the world Dylan Colman was at that moment, and she was thankful. Because her greatest fear was that, had she known where to find him, heaven and earth couldn't have kept her from running to the sanctuary of those arms.

Chapter Six

Elise gazed out the window of Keith's car as it sped down U.S. 101 toward San Francisco. She did a lot of that, she realized—looked outward from inside, almost like a sick child, who yearned not so much to join her playmates but simply to have done with being ill. Well, she was going to the doctor today like a good girl. Unfortunately, she was past the age of believing a lollipop and a kiss could make the hurt go away.

Although Dylan's kiss had certainly made her forget the pain, forget everything, for a while.

"You're awfully quiet today," Keith said.

She glanced at him in apology even as she tucked her chin to avoid too close scrutiny. She'd lavished makeup over her nose and cheekbones but knew the rosiness of her sunburn showed through. It didn't help when her cheeks became warmer with reflection on another man. "Just thinking about my appointment with Dr. Emerson," she improvised.

"I see." Keith concentrated on the road, a rueful quirk to his lips. "I didn't suppose you could be contemplating our upcoming wedding, which is the day after tomorrow." He sounded vexed, almost petulant.

"We're having such a small ceremony, I can't imagine overlooking even one detail," Elise answered, choosing to deliberately misunderstand him. The sense of guilt and betrayal increased. She was holding back from him. But why couldn't she tell Keith if not about Dylan, then about the questions and feelings he'd raised in her? Why didn't she try to seek comfort and understanding in the man she loved and was going to marry?

Because somehow, the answer occurred to her, she couldn't imagine Keith being able to give her what she needed. Not as Dylan had. And she needed time to think about the whole situation and its ramifications on the three of them: Dylan, Keith and herself.

"Aunt Char has been over the lists and instructions with me twenty times," she went on. "I don't dare think what the consequences would be if something *did* go wrong. She's almost more excited than—" Too late, Elise cut off the rest of her sentence. *The proverbial Freudian slip.* Perhaps Keith had reason to be annoyed.

"Yes, well, I'd kind of hoped *you'd* be excited," Keith said.

Elise said nothing, fiddling with the engagement ring on her finger. It was a simple setting, no diamond, just a small, oval sapphire; she'd insisted on it, claiming expensive ornaments weren't her style. Keith had wanted to give her something much more extravagant, but she'd no desire for such a . . . a complication, even before this new crop of doubts had sprung up. She eyed the ring. Had she had reservations—even then?

"Maybe I'll be more excited after today," she finally said, making the effort to confide in him. "I'm worried, Keith. About these headaches coming back when I'd thought they'd stopped. About when I'll be able to—" She couldn't tell him about being unable to paint. The fear was still too great to voice. Yet she'd told Dylan. "—when I'll be able to drive again."

He reached across and covered both her hands as they lay twined in her lap. "I know you're worried, Elise. I don't blame you for being distracted. You do know I'm very happy to drive you anywhere you want to go," he offered in assurance.

It was the same statement her aunt had made last night. *Do you really mean anywhere?* she wanted to ask. "That's not the point, Keith."

She squeezed her eyes shut, trying to repress the image of Dylan Colman that insisted on imprinting itself on her mind. *Where would you go, if you could go anywhere in the world?* His face had been so hopeful, so full of promise. So full of love. Here was the man who could take her anywhere she wanted to go.

Her head started to hurt in a place it never had before, right behind her eyes.

The pain must have shown on her face, for Keith gave her hand another squeeze. "All right, darling. I don't want to be the one to upset you. It's just that I hate seeing you so frustrated when you really don't need to push yourself. I'm afraid of how it'll affect you if the doctor thinks it's still too soon for you to do some of the things you want to."

She opened her eyes and looked at him in bewilderment. "You were the one who suggested that if my limitations were annoying me it might be a sign I needed to move on," she pointed out.

His mouth tightened in rebuke. "You certainly seem set on contradicting me today."

"I'm not—" Elise broke off. Maybe her worry *was* making her contentious. And maybe Keith could be a little more responsive, she thought with a surge of the contrariness Keith had pinned on her. Apparently the last few days with Dylan were having their effect. In any case, nothing would be solved by arguing. "All right. I shouldn't unload my nervousness on you." She searched for a change of subject that would neutralize the tension between them. "What will you do with yourself while I'm seeing Dr. Emerson?"

"I have some business to take care of in the financial district."

"A new prospect?" Keith often had inquiries from San Francisco business people looking to invest in the Sonoma Valley real-estate market.

"It's a . . . legal matter."

"Oh. Isn't your attorney in Santa Rosa?" Still fingering her ring, she noticed that in that light the sapphire lost its blue facet. Instead, it was black—a midnight black, like Dylan's eyes. Distracted, she almost missed Keith's answer.

"This guy is a different kind of lawyer," he said vaguely. At her questioning glance, he explained, "He handled my divorce."

He now had her complete attention. "But I thought you said your divorce had been finalized a year ago."

"It was."

"Then what possible reason would you have to see a divorce lawyer?" It suddenly occurred to her what his reasons might be: her assets were much less significant than Keith's—and he'd been burned once by marriage. "Is it because of us? To have a prenuptial agreement drawn up?"

His chin jutted almost obstinately. "No. There's no need for one, in my opinion. I don't plan to lose you, too, Elise," he said with a prophetic emphasis.

"Then . . . why?"

"You may as well know," he said with seeming reluctance, "since it'll come out sooner or later. I make monthly payments to Sharon."

"You mean your wife—your ex-wife?" *She* was going to be his wife, Elise reminded herself. "You pay her alimony?"

For some reason, he stiffened. "It's not alimony."

"Oh, that's right. California's a community-property state. The settlement—"

"It's not part of the settlement, either," he interrupted, as if she'd suggested something unconscionable. "I . . . choose to give Sharon this money."

Elise stared at him. "But, Keith, she deserted you!" Not until the words were out of her mouth did Elise realize how tactless the statement was. Keith didn't need it rubbed in his face that his wife had so overtly rejected him. Elise knew how it had hurt him. Still did. What must it be like to have the one you loved most in the world abandon you? She would have been devastated for years. "I—I didn't mean it like that, Keith. I just think . . . no, I know I couldn't be so forgiving. Truly, I didn't mean to suggest you wouldn't have good reason to contribute to her welfare." She searched around for one of those reasons. "Is she unable to support herself?"

"Unfortunately, Sharon's perfectly capable of taking care of herself," Keith said on a short laugh that was anything but cheerful.

Unfortunately? Puzzled, Elise again couldn't stop the question springing to her lips. "Then why would she take money from you?"

"Worried there won't be enough to go around?"

His sarcastic tone more than anything shocked her; his implication hit home with deadly accuracy. "That was completely uncalled for," she said.

He obviously realized this just as she did. "It was, and I'm sorry. I understand you're indignant on my behalf." He seemed to think through his explanation before voicing it. "Sharon's not taking advantage of me, Elise. But she was my wife. I need to know she's taken care of." He reached over for the second time that morning and took her hand.

Still puzzled, hurt by his biting remark, and vaguely troubled by his explanation, Elise didn't pull away from him, but neither did she return the pressure on her fingers. "I just can't help wondering why you didn't tell me about the arrangement with Sharon before this." *He doesn't have to tell you everything, just as you don't need to tell him your life's secrets.*

"I should have, I know. I didn't want to upset you." He hesitated. "You see, the agreement stipulates that she receive the check directly from me."

Elise began to wonder if it was just her, or was this whole conversation just a little bit bizarre. Why would his ex-wife, who'd left him, want to maintain any contact with him? Did Sharon travel all the way to San Francisco once a month just to pick up a check? "I don't know what to think, Keith. Should I be...worried?"

"You mean should you be jealous?" He looked faintly gratified by the notion. "No, darling. If anything, Sharon should be jealous of you."

Then it hit her. It wasn't Sharon who wanted to see him; it was Keith who wanted to see Sharon. But not because he still loved her. The uneasy foreboding that had been creeping up on Elise now surrounded her heart. Was that why he made payments to Sharon, so he'd have a means to remind his ex-wife of what she'd given up? A means to show her, when the time came, that the man she'd left behind had found someone else who wanted him? And why wait to tell Elise now, two days before their wedding, about the arrangement with his ex-wife, when it might be too late to...to do what? What did knowing this fact change?

A lot. For the first time, Elise pushed past the reasons she'd always told herself why Keith Hurston would want to marry her, someone struggling with the kinds of hardships—not just monetary, but also physical and emotional—that would keep her from being able to love him completely. Could it be because those same hardships might make her stay with him even without love? She wanted to ask Keith why a self-sufficient woman would consent to receiving support from a man with whom she no longer wanted any connection, except then Elise would have had to ask why she herself accepted his support. And she didn't think it had so very much to do with true love.

Or are you merely looking for a reason not to love Keith, so you'll be free to love Dylan?

Apparently interpreting her speechlessness for pique, Keith continued soothingly, "I know it must be difficult to learn that your future husband still has some contact with his ex-wife, but try to understand, Elise. You should be reassured, in fact. When I commit to love, honor and cherish someone, I take it very seriously. I made a promise to take care of Sharon and I will, just as I will you. No matter what she's done."

Elise was not the least bit reassured. In fact, she grew even more uneasy as it came to her why they were having this conversation now: because Dylan had shown up, and Keith wasn't positive there was no prior connection between her and that stranger.

What *had* she done?

No! *What had he?*

"I should have come over last night, despite your protests."

Her attention jerked back to him. "What?"

"Last night," Keith repeated. "I should have brushed aside your objections and spent the evening with you so you wouldn't have had the time to do all this worrying."

But she had needed the time—to think! And she hadn't been worried about this particular complication because she hadn't even been aware of it. "I told you, I was tired. I wouldn't have been much company. I have some things to do before Saturday." *Like sort out my life.* "Aunt Char needs me to go through the boxes of my belongings stashed away in her attic—Keith!"

Elise grabbed the armrest as the car swerved sharply for no reason. Once back in their lane, she craned her neck and peered out the rear window, expecting to see a torn piece of tire tread or other debris in the road.

"Sorry, Elise. My hand slipped." Both of them firmly on the wheel now, he moved forward in his seat. "Doesn't much boost your confidence in me, does it? You're apprehensive enough in the car without me doing something like that."

"I'm all right," she lied. Her nerves were jumpier than ever.

Keith frowned, eyes on the road. "I'd forgotten about those boxes. You know there's no reason for you to go through them before the wedding. After it either, for that matter."

She wanted to agree, to have an excuse to avoid the secrets the attic held that had terrified her so completely last night. But she had to face whatever was there. She hoped it wasn't just the light of day that strengthened her will. "There's probably papers and documents that should be put somewhere else for safekeeping, old mail— Who knows what's up there?"

"I do."

So he did. A chill went through her, that same sense of violation she'd experienced with Dylan. *He's been through all of my belongings.* Keith knew what was in the attic, would know what was there that terrified her. But he couldn't know exactly, Elise reminded herself. He'd not recognize a box of brushes or a stained palette as raising incomprehensible fear in her. No, Keith wouldn't see, as Dylan seemed able to, what secrets she hid in the deepest corners of her mind.

"I took care of whatever mail had accumulated up in Oregon," Keith explained. "And I distinctly remember telling you I was having the rest forwarded to my post-office box here in town." He meant to be reassuring. Yet, again, he was not.

"Then what's been happening to it?" It was a question she should have asked a long time ago and hadn't. "I know you went through and took care of the outstanding bills, but what about my personal mail?" With a start, she realized she hadn't received anything—a letter, a postcard, nothing—since her accident. And she knew why. She'd chosen to cut herself off from civilization. Once she recovered from her injuries enough to contemplate how her life had shattered to bits, the last thing she'd wanted to do was think about what she'd lost in the rubble. The disappointment, anger and frustration would have taken over and destroyed her just as completely as her accident had nearly done. "What about the mail addressed to me that wasn't bills?"

Keith studied her warily. "Were you expecting word from someone?"

"No..." True, she had few friends, and Charlotte was her only living relative, but it seemed as if at least one person in the world would have tried to contact her in four months.

Like Dylan. *What about my letters—*

"Elise."

She glanced at Keith, her mind an upheaval of insubstantial suspicions and uncertain accusations. He hadn't answered her question. Neither had she answered his, though.

"Is there something I should know?" Keith asked quietly.

"I don't know." She spread her hands in the air before her. "Don't you see? *I don't know.* That's why I need to go through those boxes."

He was silent a few moments before saying, his tone definite, "Believe me, there's absolutely nothing you'll need from them in the foreseeable future."

But what about the unforeseeable future? she almost asked. Or the unsettled past? "Keith, I really do appreciate all you did and continue to do to help me get over this accident, but I need to start standing on my own two feet. I've taken advantage of your patience and generosity much too long." Should one sound so formal talking to one's fiancé? "Do you realize I've never even looked at a statement of the debts you incurred on my behalf? Even though my working at the gallery has helped offset some of those obligations, I need to know the extent of them so I can pay you back."

"Don't be ridiculous. We're getting married." He'd gone back to being indulgent, pooh-poohing her concerns in that way that never failed to irritate her just a little bit. "Tell you what. After the wedding, you can write me a check."

"It's not just *money!* I'm serious, Keith." She did sound ridiculous, bringing this matter up right before their wedding, but she was desperate, she realized. Very, very desperate. She tugged at the restrictive seat belt strap across her chest. It seemed to hold her bound in a way she found suddenly intolerable. "You don't want a wife with all sorts of unresolved problems to deal with—"

"What problems?"

"Have you really not seen that for months I've been fighting for my life!"

Without warning, they plunged into darkness. Pure terror seized her throat in the instant before her eyes adjusted and she saw where they were. Keith had pulled into the cavernous parking garage under her doctor's building. She hadn't even noticed they'd entered the city. Elise spent the time in which he located a parking space striving for control over her emotions. What was happening to her? She was nearly hysterical—first last night, scaring the wits out of Aunt Charlotte, and now today with Keith. It wasn't their fault. Neither he nor Charlotte could know the extent of her ordeal, the demons that plagued her; she'd devoted a tremendous amount of energy to ensuring they were kept in the dark.

When he'd shut off the ignition, Keith turned to her. "What is all this talk of problems and not wanting you?" The dim light hid his expression from her, but his tone was soothing. "I love you, darling. Nothing could change that."

"But I need to know, Keith, before the wedding. What's in those boxes that might change me in *my* eyes."

"Then I'll say it again. I've been through everything and there are no loose ends. None. Trust me."

Elise narrowed her gaze, probing the shadowy interior of the car for a hint of that steadfastness and security she'd always found in Keith's eyes to back up his words, needing that certainty urgently right now. But there wasn't enough light.

She knew in that moment that she didn't want to trust or owe or marry Keith Hurston, not until she obtained her freedom. Freedom from her past so that she could come into a marriage whole and well. And she had the strongest hunch that was the last thing Keith wanted for her. He'd even said he loved her just as she was right now.

No matter what she'd done.

What had she been thinking—or not thinking about—these past months? *How can I find my love if I can't find myself?* She couldn't commit to anyone until...

Dylan. Since his appearance in Viento Blanco, he'd been cultivating this doubt, planting thousands of others in her mind. Or was he the Rainmaker to her Lizzie, doing what she'd feared he'd do from the first moment she set eyes on him? Had he shored her up with insubstantial hopes rather than let her dig at the weaknesses that kept her from discovering her own answers?

No. The hope he'd given her had been real. She knew because he'd challenged her when surely he knew he risked distancing her—and yet he'd drawn her closer to him. Whether he intended it to or not, his proximity, instead of making her feel confined, had made her feel more free.

Trust me. Both Dylan and Keith had asked this of her, and she was uncertain whether to give her trust to either of them. *Better the devil you know than the devil you don't.* The question was, which was which?

Elise pressed her knuckle against her right eye socket. It didn't alleviate the pressure. This pain didn't seem to be connected to her injury. Actually, it felt like a plain old tension headache. "I'm going to be late for my appointment," she mumbled as she gathered her purse and coat in her arms and avoided Keith's eyes.

"You're angry," he stated.

"No—" she started to protest, then stopped herself. "Yes, I guess I am angry."

He sighed. "I knew I shouldn't have told you about Sharon."

"That would have only postponed this discussion." And there was more to discuss. She couldn't marry him, at least not so soon, and she wanted to talk to him about rethinking their relationship, but this was neither the time nor place to bring the subject up. Neither did she want him to associate that issue with the one regarding his ex-wife, even though more than one revelation today unquestionably affected her decision. If they decided not to marry, it would be because they didn't truly love each other. Anything else could be worked out.

She turned, and something about his posture as he leaned back against the door behind him and away from her, made her ask, "Is there anything else I should know, Keith?"

Slowly, he shook his head. "No."

Yet her intuition made her suspect he hid something. *You've been hiding yourself from him, too,* a voice in her head accused. They were both guilty. The flawed honesty on which they'd based their relationship saddened her. She'd wanted to believe in the constancy of at least one part of her life.

Now, she had nothing to believe in.

Georgette Emerson entered the examining room in the purposeful manner that so characterized her personality, making Elise smile. She was a tall woman in her mid-fifties, with observant blue eyes that Elise guessed discerned far more than was ever said.

Here, actually, was the person who'd saved her life.

"Hello, Elise Nash!" Dr. Emerson cheerfully said as she took a seat on a small stool, wheeled it over to the counter and opened Elise's file.

"Hello, Dr. Emerson," Elise answered with a grin from her perch on the examination table. This had been her neurologist's standard greeting each morning when she'd entered Elise's hospital room. Elise had to admit she missed it. Even when she'd lain in a coma, it seemed she'd heard that bright salutation come through.

Dr. Emerson reviewed the file for a moment, then planted an elbow on top of the papers and turned to Elise. "Tell me. How have you been feeling?"

Elise was surprised to feel her smile die as a lump rose in her throat. "Not too great, if you want to know the truth."

"Of course I do." Dr. Emerson frowned. "I'd hoped to give you a clean bill of health today, get out of your hair for the next six months, but if you're still not feeling up to snuff, then we need to take care of it. What seems to be the problem?"

"It's the headaches, Dr. Emerson. They've come back."

"Less severe than before? More severe?"

"More—or so it seems. It's like the right side of my head's going to cave in. Or explode outward."

"And how do they start?"

"Sometimes one will come on like a hammer blow, but I've noticed some start with a dull pounding that builds up, with a final stab of pain right at the peak of the headache." Elise already felt a kind of relief just in unburdening herself. Dr. Emerson would know what to do. "I've gotten them off and on for the past three days now."

"Any other symptoms?" She waved her pencil in the air. "Dizziness? Nausea?"

"Both, in varying degrees."

"Any trouble sleeping?"

"A little, but I think it's more from worrying about this than anything else."

"Trouble concentrating?"

Elise thought about the unfinished sketch of Dylan. "Yes."

"Do you have a headache right now?"

"Yes, but it isn't like the other ones. This feels like a regular headache."

"What *is* a regular headache?" Dr. Emerson asked with a smile as she stood. "The debate continues." She flicked off the overhead light and tipped Elise's chin up to shine an ophthalmoscope, as Elise had long ago learned it was called, into her eyes. The doctor had her perform a few visual tracking exercises and did some reflex tests.

Dr. Emerson turned on the light and returned to her stool, scribbling a short note before tossing down the pencil and crossing her legs. "Well, Elise, I'm puzzled—and disappointed for you. Your last MRI was spotless. When the headaches stopped as well, we thought you were out of the woods on that head injury." She pinched her chin thoughtfully. "Is there anything that seems to provoke the onset of the headaches? Tiredness? Physical activity?"

"More like...emotional activity," Elise corrected. "I've been restless lately, feeling like I want to push myself more to do normal things. Last night I tried to drive my aunt's car. I thought my head was going to split open. The anxiety was...paralyzing." It was an effort not to shiver at the recollection."

Those observant blue eyes missed nothing. "I see. Well, we've known that's a problem, given the circumstances of your accident and how your parents died." Again, she consulted Elise's file. "Do you still remember nothing of your accident?"

Elise shook her head. "Sorry."

"No reason to be sorry. Anteretrograde amnesia, when a patient doesn't remember a traumatic incident, isn't unusual. You may never remember those few minutes right at the most frightening part of your accident. In many cases, patients can't remember the events leading up to, during and after an accident or another major shock to their system for many months, even years. The good news is we've seen some shrinkage of that window in time as you've progressed in your recovery. But because the amount of memory loss directly correlates to the severity of the concussion, it'll be more time before we can determine the extent of any permanent memory loss." She smiled in sympathy. "You did take a pretty hard knock on the head, Elise."

"But shouldn't I be remembering more of what happened by now?"

"Yes and no. It depends on the individual. In the weeks just after your accident, you were pretty much normal for someone with your injury. Once you'd come out of the coma, we asked you questions at different intervals to determine the extent of your memory loss—your name, where you were from, the current year or who's president. Most patients at that stage don't recall answering these questions, even though they might answer them correctly." Dr.

Emerson smiled. "Remember the nurse bringing you clam chowder for lunch one day, and you had no idea how she knew it was a favorite of yours?"

"I remember," Elise answered even as another memory jarred her. *How do I know these things, Elise? You told me.* Or had Dylan found out from someone else?

"If there'd been too many blank spots in your memory," Dr. Emerson went on, "then we'd have looked for more damage to the brain. From what we could determine, you had definite memory loss but it related mostly to the accident." The doctor tilted her head as she regarded Elise. "What about retrograde amnesia? Do you remember the events leading up to the accident yet?"

"Bits and pieces." Elise concentrated. "I don't remember renting the car or where, but I do remember it was raining, which is strange because I wouldn't have driven to my aunt's with rain in the forecast. Not after…I mean, how my parents died."

"You must have had an urgent reason to travel that night."

"I can't imagine what. I'd have called Aunt Char if I'd had anything really important to tell her."

"Yet your aunt had no idea you were coming or we might have been able to identify you earlier, had she filed a missing person's report."

No, Aunt Char hadn't known she was coming, Elise thought. Neither had her landlord known that she'd left. No one had known where she was or that she'd even disappeared.

Had she become that much of a recluse? The idea of existing in a world where no one was aware of whether she lived or died terrified her. Never again, Elise vowed, would she shut herself off like that from people.

"Then you don't remember why you were on your way to Viento Blanco?" Dr. Emerson prodded gently.

Elise hesitated, thinking. "I guess it was just for a visit." Yet she knew it had to be a much more important reason than that. Had she been running from something? Or someone?

Was this missing period in her life when she'd known Dylan? But how could it be—the interval of time that was still hazy to her wasn't long enough to have fallen so thoroughly in love with a man. Was it? And why would she forget only him?

Elise didn't realize how long she sat without speaking until she glanced up and found Dr. Emerson's perceptive gaze upon her.　.

"Tell you what, Elise," she said, "I'd like to schedule a few more neuropsychological tests, if you can stand it. You did so well on the last battery, I'd hoped we'd be done with them for a while. And I think it best we get you in with a good psychiatrist as soon as possible. The nature of your headaches makes me think that some of your amnesia could be more functional—psychological, that is—than organic."

"What 'functional' causes might there be?" Elise asked with a hint of alarm, still thinking of Dylan and how he might fit into this whole predicament.

"Well, your terror of driving, for example, as a function of your particular history as opposed to your accident." Dr. Emerson leaned over and began making notes in Elise's file even as she continued, "I think it's time we concentrated on dealing with that problem. I'd elected earlier to delay psychiatric counseling so you could devote your energies to recovering physically. And you seemed to be handling everything so well. But these headaches might stem more from a psychological than physical origin, even though they're exhibiting themselves physically." She glanced up. "After your parents' deaths, did you receive any kind of grief counseling?"

"No. I didn't know there was anything called grief counseling. I was only seventeen."

"But you talked to your aunt or your friends about the feelings you had about your parents' accident?"

"No," Elise repeated, feeling a little foolish. Dr. Emerson's tone took it for granted that Elise had received some sort of help.

"And besides me, you've talked to no one about your own accident, about your feelings of... whatever—fear, frustration, anger—anything that might have risen from either incident?"

"No," Elise answered a third time. She'd never talked to anyone about her parents' accident—or hers. But there was a good reason she hadn't. Both times, she felt she'd already upset Aunt Charlotte enough, and she hadn't wanted to burden the older, frailer woman with her troubles. As for talking to others about it, she'd been moved from her network of friends in Boston to Viento Blanco after her parents' deaths and hadn't even had the comfort of familiar surroundings to help her heal.

And as for talking to Keith... well, Keith had never seemed a likely confidant either, Elise admitted, to her surprise.

Yet Dylan had. Almost against her will, she'd confided in him. Trusted him.

"Tell me, Dr. Emerson," she said suddenly, "did I ever mention the name Dylan at any time after my accident? Dylan Colman?"

Dr. Emerson bit the inside of her cheek in thought. "No, I don't recall that you did, and the nurses would have noted it if you had. Sorry. Is he someone you should have mentioned?"

"I don't know." It was on the tip of Elise's tongue to pour out the incredible story of Dylan Colman. But what would she say, that she'd met a man who believed the two of them shared a previous life? That when she was with him, she felt as if she'd found some part of herself she hadn't even known she'd lost? "Is it possible to have an even more selective amnesia than just blocking out parts of a traumatic incident?"

"Such as?"

"I mean, is it possible to forget certain events or times in your life...or to forget some people but not others?"

"It's possible to have blank spots in one's memory but not the loss of identity itself, usually caused by trauma to the brain, such as in an accident like yours. But eventually the patient would become aware that there were bigger holes in their memory, beyond the normal traumatic memory loss. Has this happened to you, Elise?"

"It doesn't seem like it has, but how would I know?"

Dr. Emerson shrugged. "Over time, it would become more and more apparent to you that...something was missing. And only you can determine that, Elise. I have no other knowledge of your life or history other than what you've told me."

How do I know, Elise? You told me.

With a sudden urgency, Elise leaned forward. "I think there is something missing, Dr. Emerson. I need to know if there is."

"I'm glad you feel that way, Elise. That's often the first step to full recovery." She glanced down at her hands clasped on her lap. "However, you need to know that the reason I want to get you in with a psychiatrist is because of the possibility that your continued memory loss is at least in part...emotionally induced."

"Emotionally?"

"A mental reaction rather than being caused by an injury. Any memory loss is a result of the mind blocking out an event that was so traumatic or shocking that it must be erased from a patient's mind in order for them to function."

The doctor's words struck a chilling chord with Elise. She knew what Dr. Emerson suspected—that the headaches, that her phobia about driving, even the loss of her ability to paint, were a result of an emotional shock—what another person had done to her. Dylan? Had he done something that would cause her to block him from her memory, almost make it so he never existed? But why now and not before?

Unless it had something to do with her accident. *What had he done?* Would he do it again?

And if she'd forgotten Dylan, what or who else had she forgotten, and why?

The air in her lungs seemed obstructed, none coming in, none going out. It was the same sensation she'd felt when Dylan had first confronted her with his stories of their shared history: she had no control over her past, and therefore no control over her life.

"Elise," Dr. Emerson said softly, bringing Elise back to the present. "Are you feeling all right?"

Her hands were clammy and her heart battered the inside of her chest like the wings of an enormous bird caught in a trap, but she managed to ask, "How would I discover what I was repressing?"

"Talking about it, hypnosis, searching your mind for details that might spur your memory—but such soul-searching should be done with the help of a trained psychiatrist. That's why I want to get you in with Dr. Hathaway right away."

Dr. Emerson turned away, again intent on scribbling something in Elise's file, but she caught the other woman's air of hesitancy.

"What else do you suspect, Dr. Emerson?" Elise asked. She had to know!

The doctor looked at her, her gaze gentle with compassion. "I suspect you're hurting inside, Elise, and may have been for a long time before your accident. And I want that to stop for you."

Elise stared at her, comprehension hitting like a locomotive. "You mean hurting about things having to do with my mother or father, don't you?"

"Now, we don't know anything yet—"

"No." She shook her head in growing denial. "They were wonderful parents. They always took care of me, loved me."

"I don't want to alarm you, Elise, but you need to know we see this type of amnesia most often in cases of abuse. Basic trusts were broken sometime in one's childhood, and instead of dealing with the loved one who broke those trusts, a person will convince themselves it never happened rather than lose faith—"

"*No*, Dr. Emerson," Elise interrupted again, her voice shaking with sudden anger. "My parents did nothing to harm me, and no one will make me believe differently, especially not some shrink who doesn't even know me!"

"Elise, please." Dr. Emerson sent an open hand out to touch Elise's knee. Elise pushed the hand away. "You must know by now that I would never recommend any treatment that I didn't think would benefit you."

For long minutes, Elise resisted the possibility her doctor had brought up. It wasn't true! It couldn't be true. Not her mother and father. She'd loved them so, she would have willingly died with them that awful night seven years ago.

But she hadn't died, not then, nor four months ago. She'd survived, for whatever reasons, and she did want to live. Wasn't that why she was here?

With the aid of that hidden cache of strength, Elise managed to stem the tide of unadulterated panic that had beset her and made her lash out at Dr. Emerson—the person who had saved the life she now struggled to hold together, and the one person she trusted completely because of that. Yet there just couldn't be any way her parents might have hurt her. Fresh panic consumed her. *Please, God, no. Let it be anything, anything but that!*

But you want answers! She needed them, badly.

"Look," said Dr. Emerson, her concern obvious as she stood and pressed a button on the wall intercom, "I'm going to have my assistant call Dr. Hathaway's office right now and see if we can get you in for an appointment as soon as…Sandy, we need to—oh, wait a sec." She pulled Elise's file toward her, noticing something there. Her fingers massaged her forehead as she gave a sigh at the complication her gaze had lit upon. "I'd forgotten, Elise. I've got down that you're getting married the day after tomorrow."

"I'm not getting married, Dr. Emerson."

The older woman's professional demeanor deserted her momentarily as her mouth fell open an inch, then abruptly snapped shut. "I'll get back to you, Sandy," she said, and slowly lowered herself back onto the stool. She looked at her young patient expectantly.

Elise swallowed. "Well, I don't think it would be the most intelligent move I'd made in my life, marrying someone when I've obviously got some problems to work out." Her gaze strayed to the innocuous seascape on the wall. She pulled it back to Dr. Emerson with effort. "I need to know what's going on in this head of mine. I need to know the whole truth—no matter how painful it is."

Bright blue eyes conveyed compassion—and admiration. "The first time I saw you, Elise Nash, battered and bruised as you were, I knew you were a fighter. A survivor. The human body is a wondrous machine, the human brain a miracle of physiology, and I don't think we doctors and scientists will ever completely understand how it works. But it's the human spirit that will always confound us and humble us. I have every belief you'll be able to handle whatever your sessions with Dr. Hathaway reveal. In the meantime," she scratched what looked to Elise like an incomprehensible message across a pad, "I'm going to prescribe something that will hopefully give you a little relief from that headache pain."

She tore off the square of paper and handed it to Elise, who took it as she stood on trembling legs. Dr. Emerson stood also and caught Elise's shoulders in a squeeze of support. "I'll have Sandy get you an appointment first thing Monday. Take it easy till then, all right? See if you can get more sun. It looks good on you."

Elise's hand went to her cheek. She'd forgotten about her sunburn. Of course, Dr. Emerson, ever observant, would notice—even though Keith hadn't.

"I remember when you first came in," the doctor went on as she walked Elise to the door, "you had the loveliest golden tan even your paleness couldn't hide."

"A tan?" Elise asked in surprise.

"Mmm, hmm. All the nurses were green with envy."

But there'd still been snow on the ground in Oregon four months ago, Elise thought. Where would she have gotten a tan?

Ever consider Mexico?

Had she gone there with Dylan? Had she really been acquainted with him so intimately she'd take a romantic trip with him? But when had she known him? How much of her past was really missing? She had to find out, once and for all.

And she prayed that Dr. Emerson was right—that she was a survivor and could handle whatever pain still lay ahead for her. She also hoped it'd be worth it, because right now Elise felt she was setting herself up for certain destruction and incredible heartache.

Chapter Seven

The next day at the gallery, Elise didn't even try to pretend she wasn't watching for Dylan. She stood at the front window, arms wrapped about her middle, and stared into the murky fog as if she could call him forth through sheer strength of will.

It was Friday, and she'd last seen him Wednesday afternoon. An eternity, it seemed. Yet she'd needed that time—then. Now she needed him, Dylan.

Keith knew. Elise closed her eyes on that fresh pain. He had to know, after the way he'd acted last night. Trying to cope with the disturbing development in her recovery, she'd been silent in the car as they returned to Viento Blanco after her appointment, and she hadn't cared what he made of her silence. If there were a secret in her past, a horrible secret that concerned her and her parents...she couldn't have told Keith about it for the world. She couldn't tell anyone about it, because it wasn't true! And she needed Dylan to fill in the gaps in her memory and prove her parents' innocence. Elise needed to know what it was that *he'd* done to her. She could deal with Dylan's betrayal more than her parents'. She had to deal with it, and she would—somehow.

But the heaviness in her heart told her it wouldn't be at all easy.

Elise opened her eyes and squinted into the obscurity again. Where *was* he? She'd had no opportunity to begin even trying to find him until this morning. Last night Keith had insisted on taking his "favorite girls," as he called her and her aunt, out to dinner. Elise would rather have spent the evening calling every hotel, motel and inn up and down the coast in search of Dylan, but she'd sensed Keith had wanted to keep her in his sights. And he knew how to gain her cooperation. Aunt Char's excitement was hard not to indulge, especially when her relief that everything seemed to be back to normal, after the episode with the car, was so evident. Elise had spent the evening distracted by her worry about the possibility of her parents' mistreatment of her and by the prospect of having to talk to Keith soon about reassessing their relationship. Not to mention wondering how she'd deal with her aunt's disappointment at delaying the wedding. The dinner had been cordial on the surface, but with such deep currents of tension she thought she'd go mad from the strain on her nerves.

Yet when they'd returned home and Elise, knowing she had to do something that night to move forward with her life, had asked Keith for a few moments alone, he'd done an about-face, been nearly frantic in his haste to leave her. *He knew*—of her doubts and disenchantment with their relationship. With him. The old guilt came creeping back, and she knew much of the blame for this predicament must rest on her shoulders. Regardless of the flawed nature of his love for her, he had stood by her through one of the worst times in her life. His dependability, just knowing he was there, had shored her up innumerable times.

But such support still wasn't reason enough to marry any man. Elise lay awake half the night, knowing what she felt about Keith Hurston was guilt, knowing that she mustn't let that guilt stop her from being honest with him. And trying to reconcile whatever it was within her that could turn away the love of a man who'd never harmed her and seek instead the love of a man who might already have.

So Elise had said nothing during the evening, resolved nothing during the night. And this morning she'd arrived at the gallery, heading immediately for the small bathroom in the back room. On a hunch, she'd pulled the collar of her sweater away from her neck, checked beneath the waistband on her slacks.

The punishing fluorescence of the light had revealed the faintest of tan lines on her chest and abdomen.

She'd spent the rest of the morning making calls, trying to find Dylan, with no success. And he had yet to show up here. She chafed cold arms with even colder hands. Had he finally decided to do as she'd begged a few short days ago and leave town for good? Had he given up? Could she blame him?

He couldn't give up, not yet.

Suddenly he appeared, just as he had the first day, splitting the fog with his solidness. His realness. She saw his gaze search the gallery's window for her and she lifted one hand, not quite a wave. *I'm here!*

You came back.

The bell jangled as he entered the gallery and closed the door behind him. Her relief was like a living thing, a tangible force. God, she'd missed him! She hadn't realized how much until then; she'd wanted him to come back to satisfy a yearning in her that was more than his helping her solve the mystery in her past.

He didn't advance toward her as he had the first time. Both of them stood rooted to the floor and stared at the other as a thousand questions flew between them.

Did you want me to come back to you? Should I go now?

But where did you go? And tell me again, please, why you came back to me? I need to hear it.

The question Elise voiced first was, "Where are you staying?"

"The Pine Cone Inn, just this side of Healdsburg," Dylan immediately answered. "Hurston made it clear staying in Viento Blanco would be suicide, or I would have—so I could be close to you."

"I'm glad his threats haven't stopped you from seeing me," she said.

"No one could do that, Elise."

She wanted to ask where he'd been all morning, if he ached to be with her as badly as she wanted to be with him, but she'd been the one to push him away. And she still needed to keep a distance between them. She had to find out what he'd done.

He guessed her thoughts, answering her unasked question. "I was waiting for some people to return my phone calls. I needed answers."

They both did. "Did you get them?"

"To a certain extent." His black eyes were shuttered, watching her. "Were you afraid, Elise?"

"Afraid?"

"That I wouldn't come back to you?"

She nodded, resisting any impulse to evade the issue. She couldn't do it, not when she wanted the truth desperately and so owed him the same. "It doesn't seem possible to doubt you'd return when here you stand in front of me and this...presence of yours fills the room." One arm hugged her middle even tighter, while the other slid upward across her body and her fingers rubbed the side of her neck with tense pressure. "But you're still so new in my life, Dylan, and I'm not a naturally trusting person. Without almost constant proof that you're not only here but here to stay, I do doubt you. It's been a lot of the problem between us."

"I can see that...now." Frustration rimmed his mouth, bracketing it with deep lines. "I don't know what else to say or do, Elise. I'd keep you with me every minute if I could, and not just to convince you I mean what I say. But I can't, and you won't let me, so you'll have to trust me." He raised his open hand, a gesture of trying to find expression for his thoughts. For a moment he held it so, then his fingers closed into a fist. "I told you I'd come back. I'll always come back. Believe what you must about me, but never doubt that one thing."

His gaze bore into her, not asking her to believe but making her do so. He had that power—when he was here. Elise turned away from him, trembling with the intensity of the emotion flowing between them. It was too strong to ignore or escape or to fight or deny, and because of that she knew he also had the power to hurt her. He *had* hurt her. And she had to know why.

"What is it, Elise?" She could hear his own barely contained fear in his voice. "You said you needed time to think. What have you come up with to explain our feelings for each other?"

His tone—slightly accusing—stung, made her indignant and fed her courage. "So you can negotiate your way around my argument?" she asked pointedly.

"No. The truth never needs to be negotiated."

She pivoted to face him. "Then tell me, once and for all, what it is you did to me! How did you hurt me?"

His eyes widened, his face drained of color. "What makes you think I hurt you, Elise?"

"You know me, but I don't remember you. I've blocked you from my mind for some reason, and it's got to be because of something you did to me." She took a step toward him, her anger growing apace with her dread at what his answer would be—*must* be! *He* had hurt her, caused this chaos, not her mother or father. "What did you do?" she asked again.

"I don't know, Elise. What do you think I did?"

"I want to know if my accident really was an accident. What really happened that night? Everything was burned to a cinder—the car, any identification that might have told someone who I was. My aunt had no idea I was coming, my landlord had no idea I'd left town." She pressed the pads of her fingers to her closed eyes, searched her mind one more time for the wisp of a remembrance or explanation. Behind her eyelids, she found nothing but blackness. "Where was

I going that night, Dylan? I still don't know." Her hands fell
to her sides and she probed his own penetrating gaze. "Or
maybe the question is, where was I being taken?"

She could see she'd shocked him with her insinuations.
No, not shock—his eyes filled with hurt. Deep hurt. She recalled their first meeting, when she'd seen the same expression on his face: as if she had hurt *him*. It was the last thing
she wanted to do, she realized. She'd never wanted to hurt
him, because she loved—

"Elise." Now Dylan took a step forward and the space
between them closed to less than a yard. "I had nothing to
do with your accident. I wasn't even on the same continent
when it happened."

He was asking her to trust him—again. Yet he'd still given
her nothing but generalities. And she couldn't trust him, not
yet. Not again.

How she wanted to, though. Every instinct in her yearned
for him and the certainty in his eyes. Perhaps, she thought,
it was more a matter of trusting herself.

"Tell me, then," she finally said. "What's *your* explanation of this whole situation?"

"I'm as much in the dark as you. That's why I spent all
yesterday calling in every favor I'd ever done. I talked to
some of the best military physicians and specialists in the
country, grilled them on every conceivable possibility of
what happened and why."

"And what did you come up with?" she asked. Could it
be he had the answer that would set them both free?

She saw in his eyes that he didn't. "I told you once that
I'd never hurt you, Elise. I couldn't hurt you, but somehow I have—or you think I have. Somehow, you've concluded I did or didn't do...something, and I broke your
trust."

So he *had* hurt her. What he said followed the exact pattern Dr. Emerson had described as causing functional amnesia. Sometime in her past, she'd wanted to believe in this
man, had believed in him, and he'd forsaken her trust in

him. Only someone she'd loved greatly could have caused such a disruption in her life.

And so, too: she had loved him. The admission set loose a despair that sounded the very depths of her soul.

Because she still loved him, no matter what he'd done.

Elise bent her head, knowing she must have the complete truth. "What did you do?"

"As I said before, I don't know. But I've come to the conclusion that it isn't what *I've* done to breach your trust that's made you forget me."

At his words, her body set itself to trembling as if an earthquake shook the floor. For a moment, it seemed one had actually hit, for a powerful disorientation overtook her, causing her stomach to churn.

"I talked to five doctors yesterday, Elise, trying to figure it out. All I know is you shared some of your most intimate secrets with me, yet you never told me how your parents died—"

"No!" Her head snapped up. "They didn't do anything wrong to me! They loved me! I don't care what you or Dr. Emerson say, it isn't true!" Her lungs constricted and she gasped for breath like one drowning. "They'd never hurt me," she still managed to whisper.

She saw the weight of her words strike and comprehension sink in. "You mean...? God, Elise."

Again, Elise spun away from him, shutting out the look on his face. An inferno of shame burned in her, and she gathered what resources she could to extinguish it. It wasn't true! *Oh, Mom...Dad...*

She wished for aloneness—an island, a mountaintop, or some kind of anonymity in a world that had invaded her privacy and had become much too intimate with her. But that was how she'd failed before, by shutting herself away.

Strong arms went around her from behind, and for a split second she felt trapped. Then the warmth of those arms enveloped her, seeped in. Freed her.

"Elise, truly, I never thought you'd suffered that kind of harm. I still don't." His jaw was pressed against the right

side of her head, the side that always hurt. It didn't right
now. "I mean, some of the doctors suggested childhood
abuse, but in my gut I just didn't think that was it. If there's
a connection between your parents and your not remembering me, I can't help thinking it's a perception you've
reasoned out in your subconscious, because," he turned her
to face him, "I know I haven't hurt you that way, Ellie. Believe me, I could never do something you'd even begin to
connect to that sort of experience in your past." His fingers tightened on her upper arms. "There's got to be some
other reason you can't remember me. And we *will* find out
what that is."

Elise looked up at him, into his deep-set eyes. Steely conviction and purpose emanated from him in waves. She believed him, because what he said made sense. She found
hope, because he believed that the truth could be endured.
And she found courage, because he would face that truth
with her.

Into his open arms she went. This was what her heart had
been seeking for an eternity: this understanding, this
strength, this commitment. This man. This love.

She wasn't alone any longer. They were in this together.

Elise raised her chin in sudden urgency. "Dr. Emerson
said to talk about what happened, search for words or things
that might spur my memory."

"I've tried, hoping *you'd* tell *me* what happened."

"I know. We just haven't hit on the right detail." She
thought furiously for a moment. "Bringing those different
foods the other day was good, even if I didn't flash on anything specific. When we went sailing, I almost felt...
something. What else did we do together, Dylan?"

He let her go and stepped backward, picking up a shop-
ping bag she hadn't even noticed he'd brought with him. He
reached inside and drew out a dress of gauzy, flowing material.

It was red.

"It's not exactly the same, but it's close enough," he said.

"Close to what?"

"The one you bought in Mexico. The one you wore the last night we spent together."

Her hands shaking, Elise reached out for the dress. Without a word, she walked to the back room and entered the small bathroom. She undressed, her slacks pooling at her feet as she stepped out of them. Her sweater landed on top of them. She slipped the dress on.

The fit was perfect—but then it wasn't a close-fitting dress. The waist and top were elastic, and she instinctively arranged the neckline over her upper arms so her shoulders were exposed. The skirt was long and flowing, casual and sexy. Ideal for tropical weather. She didn't remember ever owning anything like it.

Elise turned and found her image in the mirror. Even in the harsh light, even without a golden tan, she was striking in a way she'd never imagined she could be. She, the artist, had never seen how this color could bring out the highlights in her hair, warm her skin tone, accent the amber in her eyes. She looked . . . vibrant; everything about her had more depth. It was as if she looked at someone else, and she realized that she did.

This was the woman Dylan Colman had fallen in love with.

"Elise."

She swung around and opened the door. Dylan stood a few feet away, his shoulder leaning against the wall. At the sight of her he straightened. He said nothing as his gaze did a slow, thorough perusal of her before his eyes came back to hers.

"Do you remember?" he asked.

"No," she answered, "but I . . . know certain things."

"Such as?"

Elise smoothed her hands over the insubstantial material, so out of place in this damp, chilly weather. Yet she was perfectly at home in the dress. "I know that this feels . . . right," she said haltingly, staring into the dim recesses of the windowless room behind him, thinking very hard, searching her heart for complete honesty. "I know that *I* feel right—better, more whole. I know…that you love me. I know,'' her gaze shifted and found him, ''that I love you.''

He didn't move, except for his eyelids, which drifted closed. His face was immobile, composed. Tranquil as one who prayed. Then he opened his eyes and found her.

Two steps each and they were wrapped in the other's arms. Lips met without error, opened and clung.

Elise could not get enough of him, nor Dylan of her—he told her so in the way his fingers tightened in her hair, angling her mouth one way as he slanted his own the other way in a delicious counterpoint. She felt the tug of his kiss at the very center of her being.

They were both mad for precious contact as tongues matched movements and spirits soared in shared communion. And fragile remembrance stole through her: she *did* know Dylan—or did she simply want to believe, once again, that they had lived and loved before, because she loved him now?

For the moment, it didn't matter. All that counted was the very realness of him. Her hands splayed on the solid plane of his chest before crawling upward to experience the woof and warp of his sandpapered throat and jawline. He was all glorious texture, and she pulled away just long enough to find the sensuous curve of his strong mouth with her fingertips. Not a smile, exactly, but as she traced his lips, she found reassurance that, indeed, she could make him happy, could fulfill the need in him as he did in her.

Eyes dark with a languid heat, Dylan took the pad of one fingertip between his teeth, scoring it gently. Elise gasped before removing her hand and replacing it with her own hungry lips.

Deeper and finer grew his onslaught of her senses. His own exploration of her seemed as exhaustive, with the warm pressure of his hands sliding over her back, her waist, her hips. The pumping of his heart was like a drumbeat, sending out a primeval message that needed no modern translation: *We're here. Now. Together.*

She tore her mouth from his. "Tell me," she urged him. "Tell me now." But then, missing his kisses, she tugged him down for more before he could answer.

He met her need, then broke the kiss and stared down at her. "Tell you what?" Dylan rasped.

"Everything. Anything. What happened—to us."

His gaze searched hers for assurance that he wouldn't cause her harm, and Elise moaned—not in pain, but at this man's incredible compassion—and, again, pulled his mouth against hers.

This kiss was tantalizing, all lips and gliding pressure, an agony to end. But finally Dylan did on a shaky breath. The look on his face was relieved and apprehensive at once. "What happened? We met on the Mexican Riviera almost five months ago. I'd gone there for a break before this six-month stint in Saudi. You'd gone there because ... it was a beginning, you said."

Elise rubbed the outside of her thumb against his jaw, fingers buried in the hair at his nape, and studied him in puzzlement. What beginning? She calculated quickly. Five months ago—that would have been just a few weeks before her accident. What had been her mission, one that had nothing to do with Dylan, that would make her travel to a spot far away from her home for a beginning? What had she been running from?

No. With a flash of insight, Elise knew she'd been seeking, not running away. But what? Was it more the journey, not where she went, that had been significant?

"Did I ever say what that beginning was?" she asked.

Dylan shook his head. "And I never pursued it, I'm sorry to say. After the first few days of knowing you, I guess I formed my own conclusions. I wanted to believe that it was our beginning that had called you there."

His arms tightened around her as his gaze drifted over her features. "It *was* fate or destiny, whatever you want to call it, that brought us together. I'll always believe that. It hit like a lightning bolt, something I'd never felt before with a woman. And I could tell you felt it too, even though—" his eyes shifted downward, away from hers "—I knew you still had doubts."

"About . . . us?"

"I think so," Dylan mused. Elise saw in the pensiveness of his expression that he'd had no doubts about the two of them, and hers had tormented him—and still did. "I told myself it was to be expected," he continued, "because things were moving so quickly between us. Still, at the end of our two weeks together, I asked you to marry me, right away. I didn't see how I could be away from you for six months— that's how it works with my job. I'm committed night and day for a certain period of time. No vacations. No time off. And visitors aren't allowed, not in this environment. Spouses, children, yes." He lifted his gaze. "I wanted to take you with me as my wife.

"But you wouldn't commit, not so soon. I . . . understood, made myself believe that if the love was strong between us, we could survive the separation. The timing couldn't have been worse, but it was impossible to get out of my commitment. Duty called. So I went, and let you go. I just hoped I wouldn't regret it."

Yet clearly, he did. *He hadn't wanted to leave her.* Knowing how he felt about his vocation, moved by his dedication, realizing the quandary he'd faced, Elise drew his head down and pressed her cheek to his to telegraph her own regret. "I'm so sorry, Dylan," she whispered.

He held her close. "It wasn't your fault."

"No, I mean I'm sorry for what you went through. I can't imagine what it must have been like to discover—"

"Yes . . . that you'd disappeared." He brought her closer still, as if he would abide no further separation. "I didn't know anything was wrong for a month or so—only that, after the first few, my letters weren't being answered. I thought for a while that it was simply a case of slow mail. Then I wondered if I'd somehow been mistaken about us— I wrote more letters, asking you what had changed." His breath was warm against her temple as he spoke, his voice pitched low. "I tried to call you, but there was never an answer. Then when I called and found the phone had been disconnected, I *knew* something was wrong. And I couldn't let you go without trying to uncover the real truth of what had happened.

"I tried to find you, Elise—God knows how I tried. Even with connections, do you know how hard it is to locate someone from thousands of miles away?"

She shook her head, gently bumping his chin, afraid to speak as her heart became even more full with the testimony of Dylan's love for her.

"I called on family and friends to make inquiries that produced nothing. My father even travelled to Oregon to try to find you for me. Finally I faced a possibility I'd resisted from the first—that you'd *wanted* to disappear without a trace. Whether you hid from me or the doubts that hung between us, or even doubts or problems you'd had outside of our relationship, I didn't know. All I knew was you were gone and if I wanted to find you, I'd have to do it myself. I managed to get two weeks' leave to try to clear the situation up. Damn near half of it was spent in Oregon. And when I finally tracked you to Viento Blanco...it seemed you'd wiped all traces of me from your life."

Slowly, Elise pulled away from him as a terrible possibility took root in her mind. "I didn't mean to disappear," she said. "At least, I don't think I did. It doesn't...*feel* like I wanted deliberately to disappear. But maybe...someone else wanted it to seem that way."

Dylan scrutinized her briefly before her implication sank in. "Hurston?"

"I never received a letter from you because all my mail went to his post-office box. He was the one who went to Oregon and took care of all my affairs, moved all my things. He said my landlord had filed a missing-person report—"

"When?"

"About a month or so after my accident, once the due date for my rent came and went without him receiving a check. Until then, he hadn't realized I'd disappeared. No one had."

"I didn't contact the local authorities until some time after that," Dylan mused out loud. "I could get absolutely nothing out of them, and it always seemed to me they'd been . . . I don't know. Warned. If it hadn't been for a friendly postal clerk in town, I'd never have had a clue where to find you."

They both stood deep in thought, puzzling out the sequence of events. Then their eyes met in consternation. And suspicion.

"When did you and Hurston become engaged?" Dylan asked.

"A few months ago—" She looked up at him in shock. "Right after he returned from Oregon."

They both jumped at the sound of bells from the showroom. Their jangle, made discordant by the front door's forceful opening and closing, augured the arrival of someone in a great hurry. Or a great deal of turmoil.

"Elise!"

Dylan's gaze met hers—and hardened. "Speak of the devil," he murmured.

Elise laid a cautioning hand on his arm, *Let me handle this*. She stepped around him to the doorway leading to the front room.

Keith stood next to the counter, his expression ominous, though relief suffused his features at the sight of her, like a child finding the mother he'd lost in a crowd. She felt a twinge—guilt, again—that she stifled.

And she pushed back the anger that swept up on her like a tidal wave, because she needed control. She needed answers: What had he done?

"There you are—" Keith frowned. "What've you got on?"

Elise looked down at herself, her fingers, rock steady, tracing the shirred neckline. She was glad to see how calm she could be. But then, she was getting answers she'd long been searching for, the puzzle was completing itself—and it didn't seem, yet, that the truth would be so hard to bear.

"I thought I'd try something different," she said. "Do you like it?"

"It's different, all right," he muttered, casting a glance around the room, as if looking for someone. "A little cool out, wouldn't you say, for that kind of thing?"

"Actually, I was thinking of what sort of clothes I'd need if we were to take a trip to say... Mexico."

His gaze whipped to hers. "Who's going to Mexico?"

She lifted her shoulders. "Who knows?" Out of the corner of her eye she saw Dylan, still hidden from Keith, move closer to the doorway and to her. She guessed that Keith suspected Dylan had returned to Viento Blanco, and that's why he was here. Right now, she had no idea what Keith would do if he found Dylan had come back. No, she didn't know the man who stood across the room from her with fear and accusation in his eyes.

Elise propped a hip against the doorjamb, the front of her shoulder pressed against the back of it, her arm out of Keith's sight. She reached out with her hand and felt the warm pressure of Dylan's fingers as they clasped hers. She returned the pressure briefly before pulling her hand away, gesturing with a flick of her wrist toward the hidden back entrance to the gallery. *Go!*

She heard a very soft, very definite, "Like hell I will."

Elise suppressed an exasperated huff and went on, "Something draws me to the sun—or at least a place different from here. Lately I've felt this need to get away. Viento Blanco isn't for everyone." Elise looked at her fiancé, truly regretful for what she knew she must say to him. "If I leave Viento Blanco, Keith, it's because I don't see myself living here—with you."

"Who've you been talking to, Elise?" he accused.

"You, Keith," she shot back. "Does it have to be someone else who's created the problems between us?" She had to take the offensive, keep the suspicion from coming around to Dylan—because Dylan wasn't the problem. Not right now. "I've been thinking a lot in the past few days, especially since our conversation yesterday in the car. With this new spate of headaches and what Dr. Emerson's been telling me about my memory loss, especially before the accident—and after—I've started wondering about some things."

"Like what?" he asked warily.

"I've been wondering about the reasons I resisted pushing myself more to become self-sufficient and take responsibility for my life again. I can see now that I willingly allowed you to run interference for me, protect me, and you must believe that I'll always be grateful for that. But gratitude isn't a reason to marry someone, Keith. I found comfort in leaning on you, even needed it—then. Now I need to get back out into the thick of things. Get on with my life. I *am* fighting for it, as I said yesterday—fighting to be a different woman than the one you fell in love with."

"This is Dr. Emerson's doing. I could see you were upset yesterday—"

"No, Keith. We can't lay blame, any of us, just to find an answer." These were her words, spoken as Dylan crouched in front of her a few days ago. "It's nothing anyone did. Dr. Emerson, you, me—" *Dylan*. "It was an accident. An unfortunate accident."

She had her answer: there was no reason.

"The last thing any of us needs is to lay blame," she said softly, "but if we must, then blame me. No one's really known what I've been dealing with. I hid so many of my thoughts and feelings from you and Aunt Char, and it was because I was deathly afraid that you'd both find me too much a burden and...I guess I thought you'd abandon me." She paused, wondering at the vague sense that these words held deeper significance. "Dr. Emerson thinks it's time I dealt with those fears, and I think I'm finally ready to do just that."

"But I'd never have deserted you when you needed me. I told you, Elise, I love you, no matter what."

"No matter what I've done, is how you put it." But it *was* nothing she'd done. Chance had made her the victim of an accident—yet had she been a victim of a more deliberate transgression? "What about what you've done, Keith? What about what you've hidden from me?"

There was a split second in which Elise saw an intense apprehension streak across Keith's face before he scowled defensively. "Did that stranger come back?" he asked, not answering her questions. He moved closer to her with purposeful steps and her heart leapt to her throat, lest Dylan believe her threatened and come to her aid. "Sheriff Roswell's still got an eye out for him, and if he sees that guy he's got orders to lock him up, no questions asked."

Desperately, Elise gestured to Dylan in another command, the downward thrust of her closed fist. *Please! Go!* If Keith found Dylan here, he'd really clam up on her and she might never discover what he knew.

"That'll only postpone the inevitable. You must realize I'd find out eventually why Dylan came to Viento Blanco and what he knows."

"How do you know his name?"

She could have cut her tongue out. "He told me, remember?"

"I remember." Keith scrutinized her, and she hoped her expression had the right touch of forthright inquiry. "I never saw that man before he showed up a few days ago," he said, "if that's what you're asking. Regardless, I think it's more important to find out what *you* know—or should I say don't know—about him. You said you'd never seen him before, either. Is there some reason I shouldn't believe that's still true?"

She had to be honest with Keith—there'd been enough lies—but she would have given anything not to have to say her next words. "I didn't know him either. I still don't." And that was the truth, for as much as she loved Dylan, believed in him and trusted him, the past he told her of remained unrecollected by her battered brain.

Her heart ached with immeasurable regret. She stretched her hand out, seeking Dylan, wanting to reassure him. *I do love you. I do believe in you.* But she still didn't know him. There was no responding touch.

Her answer apparently reassured one man. "Look, Elise," Keith began, his voice taking on that patiently patronizing tone she realized she greatly despised, "I know you're under a lot of pressure, what with the headaches and Dr. Emerson's pushing you so hard."

Elise elbowed herself upright, away from the doorjamb. "She's not pushing me!"

"Well, obviously something is bothering you, when you really shouldn't have the strain on your nerves. Why don't I take you home so you can spend the rest of the day relaxing? I don't need my bride showing up with rings under her eyes—"

She stared at him in shock. "Surely I've made it evident there'll be no wedding tomorrow—"

"But we can't postpone it." Anxiety infused his voice. "We've got to be in Asilomar next week," he pointed out irrelevantly. "Both of us."

Her sixth sense sharpened and honed in on that anxiety, making her suddenly suspicious. "Where does Sharon live these days, Keith?"

He took a step back, as if that intuition spooked him. "She's been living in Monterey." Near Asilomar. So he really did intend to show off his new wife.

Elise had always believed that Keith's ex-wife had left him to abide in the sunny climes of Southern California. Yet if Sharon had gone only as far south as Monterey, with its mist and fog and cold, then there had to be another reason she'd escaped from Viento Blanco.

The same reason Elise wanted to escape this place, and it was to get away from the control of this man.

"I am not going to marry you, Keith," she said.

"But why? You just said you didn't know that stranger... Nothing's changed, Elise."

"Yes, it has! *I've* changed!" she cried.

"You're getting hysterical again—"

"No!" She'd never felt more sane. "I wasn't myself for a long, long time, Keith, but I'm finally getting back to being me."

"And I told you, I still love you. I want to marry you. Tomorrow, just as we've planned all along."

"But I don't love you," she said, not caring how thoughtless it sounded. Yet she made herself pause, tried to find a way to soften her message while still trying one last time to make Keith understand. "And I don't see that you really love me. Real love doesn't have its roots in dependency, compensating for each other's weaknesses. It's wanting the other person to be strong, helping them to be strong, so that the love between you has a chance to survive—to endure, even when everything conspires to tear you apart."

Now she hoped Dylan hadn't left, because she wanted him to hear the message that was for him, this declaration of her love.

Keith had his own interpretation of her words. "This *is* about Sharon, isn't it?" he asked. "Dammit, I *knew* I shouldn't have told you—"

"Yes, this is about Sharon! It's about all the things we've hidden from each other, the things we've hidden from ourselves these past four months..."

In the attic.

Elise felt the same sensation she'd experienced a few days ago, a wave of heat sweeping over her. As before, the hair on her neck rose as perspiration sheened her forehead.

This—*this* was where the answer to her questions lay. And perhaps the key to her memory.

She glanced up, this discovery and a thousand questions on her lips—and stoppered the impulse at the last instant. Keith watched her, his gaze vigilant. In a way, she'd allowed him to put her in a box—a nice, safe box whose four sides had comforted her with their familiarity and reliability in keeping the world at a distance. That was likely why he'd forgotten about the crates in the attic these past few days—a variant of "out of sight, out of mind." *Out of sight, out of memory.* She'd subconsciously erased them rather than deal with the threat contained in them.

But now she wanted to know. Now she wanted out of the box built around her.

And Keith would never tell her the truth contained in the boxes in Aunt Char's attic. No one would. She had to find out what was in them herself.

A sluggish pounding began, deep within her brain.

"Maybe I should go home," she said. Whether from dreading the headache coming on or the secrets she was about to uncover, a definite anxiety was making its presence known. She concentrated on subduing it before it had the opportunity to grow.

Keith nodded his approval. "I'm sure once you've had a chance to rest, you'll feel calmer and we can talk about this whole matter in a reasonable manner."

"Whatever." He could think what he wanted. She just had to get home, get to those boxes before this headache reached its peak.

Elise had started purposefully for the front door when Keith's "Ah, Elise—shouldn't you change?" stopped her.

"Oh, I forgot." She glanced down at the gauzy red dress. *Dylan.* She had to tell him about the boxes, wanted him with her to face what she was about to discover. "I'll just throw my coat on over this," she said, wanting to maintain whatever fragile connection she and Dylan had already established. Because she felt it slipping away as it always did when he was not in her presence.

Anxious to reestablish even a glimmer of that closeness, Elise turned and walked to the back room. Once there, she peered intently into the darkness, searching for a movement.

But Dylan was gone. She was relieved and anxious at the same time. For once again, she had to trust that this man would come back.

Hidden among the shadows, Dylan watched the couple leave the gallery, locking up behind them. Her golden hair was tucked into her drab-colored coat, snuffing its brightness. Yet he could see the barest fringe of red around the coat's hem, incongruent with the dark-colored hose and simple flats she wore. She walked ahead of Hurston, pulling up her collar as she did so. He thought he saw the covert shifting of her gaze, as if she scouted the empty street.

For him. She was looking for him.

He pressed back against the side of the building as they crossed toward him. Dylan saw Hurston reach out to take her arm. Elise moved away from that touch. Hurston shoved his fists into the pockets of his overcoat.

Dylan watched them pass by, neither knowing he was but a few steps away and praying for any excuse to reveal himself, finish the confrontation between Hurston and himself that had begun a few short days ago, and take Elise to the place she really belonged—with him. Forever.

He hadn't wanted to leave her there in the gallery to face Keith Hurston alone, but she was all right, or so he had made himself believe. He'd left at her second gesture of dismissal, although he wouldn't have, had he not felt she was handling the situation. She needed to handle it, to break off with Hurston by herself. Dylan was glad she wanted to. Glad that she wasn't marrying Hurston.

Because she loved him, Dylan Colman.

She loved him, and he felt a curious mixture of relief and dread at that revelation, because the same obstacle blocked their path as it had five months ago: Obviously, Elise still had doubts. Because she still didn't remember him.

After all his conversations yesterday with the doctors, he believed he'd hit upon the source of those doubts. The theory he'd developed on why and how she'd suppressed memory of him was one that he could live with, but what if he was wrong? What if Elise couldn't live with it, even after she remembered? And she had to remember soon—very soon. He'd only been able to break away from his assignment because he swore he'd be back at the end of two weeks, no matter what he found. That time was up in three days. Again, he wanted to take Elise with him—as his wife. He didn't think he could stand leaving her again, but he'd have to if she didn't remember, because he couldn't marry her with this obstacle between them, regardless of whether she loved him.

Yet, Dylan thought with a twisting in his gut, what if she did remember and her doubts remained? And because of them, what if she couldn't love him?

Chapter Eight

Elise ascended the steps to her aunt's front porch. She paused for a moment, fingers grasping the door handle, to discipline her features. Then she glanced over her shoulder and gave Keith what she hoped was one of her old grateful smiles.

"Thanks for seeing me home," she said, and the outdated phrase struck a dissenting chord in her. But then, their relationship had always been outdated. Antiquated for a couple in the nineties. Keith had promised her security, taken care of her, as he'd been taking care of Aunt Charlotte and her concerns for years, and Elise had wanted him to. It had probably been the most important factor in her decision to marry him—that, and the underlying goal of never letting another person too close to her. Keith had fit the bill—then, but no more.

What would happen to Aunt Char? Elise wondered suddenly. Her breaking off with Keith would surely strain the arrangement her aunt had with him. Well, it was an unfortunate side effect, but she couldn't marry a man simply to avoid upsetting her aunt. Elise would find a way to take care of her aunt's worries. Or, she reasoned, recalling the pale but resolute woman with a fireplace poker in her hand, Aunt Char would find a way to take care of herself.

Elise forced the smile that had dimmed at her thoughts and hoped they hadn't shown. "You were right, Keith. I could use some rest." She opened the door, hoping he wouldn't try to kiss her goodbye. With the taste of Dylan's kiss still on her lips, she didn't think she'd be able to hide her distaste at Keith's touch. "Thanks again," she said in dismissal.

Keith reached out behind her, his hand spreading on the face of the door. She stiffened reflexively at the pressure of his arm across the back of her shoulders. "I thought I'd come in for a few minutes," he said.

"There's no reason you should," Elise said, a little too quickly. She pressed her fingertips to her temple in an evident gesture of discomfort. "I'm afraid I won't be much company, since I plan to take one of those pills Dr. Emerson gave me and lie down in a dark room for a while."

"I'll just make sure you get settled," Keith said, his manner solicitous, but Elise detected the undercurrent of tension. They were both hiding things again. Still.

"Well, what are you two doing here in the middle of the day?" Aunt Charlotte stood in doorway, smiling at them in delight. "Playing hooky? I don't blame you. I don't have a coherent thought in my head myself, with all the excitement about tomorrow."

"I know, Aunt Char," Elise agreed, hoping to enlist her unwitting aid. "I felt a headache coming on and wanted to nip it in the bud. All I want right now is quiet, complete quiet."

Charlotte, the dear woman, reacted just as Elise anticipated she would. "Heavens! You simply can't get sick right before your wedding! We need to get you into bed right away." Leaving Keith standing at the threshold, she took Elise's arm with gentle insistence and bustled her up the stairs to the small room Elise had called her own these past few months. There, her aunt folded down the coverlet, all the while clucking assurances. "Now you get your coat and shoes off and lie down here and I'll be back in a jiffy with a cold compress for your forehead—"

"Aunt Char," Elise interrupted, "what I need is a glass of water so I can take one of the pills Dr. Emerson gave me. Right away." The pounding had escalated to a persistent hammering that was still bearable, but wouldn't be much longer if it got any worse.

Her aunt straightened abruptly. "Oh! Yes, of course." She hurried out of the room.

Still in her raincoat, Elise crossed the hall to the bathroom and snatched up the prescription bottle next to the sink. She shook a single tablet into her palm, then hesitated. The recommended dosage was one pill. If the drug had to be prescribed, it was probably pretty effective without doubling the dosage. She snapped the cap back on the bottle, resisting temptation. Yet she couldn't afford to have this headache take over. She needed to get into those boxes.

On that thought, she stepped into the hallway. At the end of it was the door to the attic. Putting the tablet on her tongue, she tipped her head back and with difficulty downed the pill dry. Then she started for the attic door.

"Elise."

She spun around. Keith stood at the head of the stairs.

"How's the headache?" he asked, gray eyes obscure as the mist outside.

"It's...about the same," she answered, her heart rising in her chest to lodge with the pill which had not gone all the way down and caused a burning sensation in her esophagus. She swallowed. "I was just going to get an extra blanket from Aunt Char's room," she lied.

"Oh, child, let me do that," exclaimed Aunt Charlotte, who'd come up the stairs and now sidestepped around Keith as he remained rooted in the middle of the hall. She handed the compress and glass of water to Elise, who gratefully took a few gulps.

"Now, Keith," Charlotte continued, her voice muffled as she searched in her closet for the requested blanket, "you

needn't worry about Elise. She's in good hands with me."
She came out of her room, the folded blanket over one arm.
"Run along, young man. You've likely got things to do before tomorrow, and I wouldn't mind one last chance to take care of my niece before she becomes your bride."

Charlotte smiled wistfully, and despite the imminence of her pain and her apprehensions, Elise smiled back at her.

"I appreciate your help, Charlotte," Keith spoke up. Both women looked at him. He hadn't moved. "But I think I'll stick around a while anyway."

"That would be lovely! I'll put a pot of coffee on and we can chat downstairs. And we'll both be within calling distance if you need anything, dear," she told Elise.

Elise could see that wasn't what Keith had in mind. His eyes darted to the attic door behind them. Obviously, he didn't want to leave her alone so that she'd have the opportunity to go through those boxes, yet he had no reason to remain up here with her—not if he wished to maintain this covert little pretense that all was well between the two of them.

She caught his eye, and he and Elise stared at each other in a sudden contest of wills. This time she wasn't backing down.

"I'm ready," she said softly. "Let's do it. Let's get it out in the open, deal with whatever it is that's feeding these weaknesses in us, keeping each of us from finding happiness within ourselves. Let's deal with our problems, Keith, like adults who at least respect, if not love each other."

"If you respected me even a little bit you'd trust me. And you wouldn't go up in that attic."

"But I already know, Keith."

"Know what?"

"What you've hidden from me." Indignation fueled her attack. She handed the compress and glass to her confused-looking aunt and stepped in front of her, wanting to shield Charlotte from at least the virulent aspect of Keith's face. "I'll admit I don't have all the details, but you knew Dylan Colman had to mean something to me. You had to know his name from the return address on his letters to me, the ones you've been collecting for the past four months.''

He blanched. "How do you know that?"

"We figured it out after—"

"So he did come back!" he interrupted harshly. "By God, I'll have him put away for good."

"Keith, forget about that for now! Let's deal with the fact that you deliberately withheld from me any indication that this man had been a part of my life. Even setting aside the moral ramifications, what you did was illegal. I could have *you* arrested for keeping my mail from me."

"But you never mentioned him, not once!" he countered. "What was I supposed to think? I thought he must be some guy you met on vacation and had an affair with, who obviously wanted to continue the romance even though you didn't."

"You couldn't know what I wanted!" she flashed back at him. The pill must have worked; her headache had decreased, enough so she was able to concentrate her energies on getting to the bottom of this matter. "You never asked!"

"I didn't have to! I figured if you really loved him, you'd have said so." Keith's gaze flickered toward Charlotte, who had moved from behind Elise and whose own gaze was shifting from his face to her niece's in concern at their heated exchange. Elise laid a soothing hand on her arm. She didn't want to put Aunt Charlotte in the middle again, but neither would Elise allow herself to back down for that reason. Keith, she noticed, registered the comforting gesture and its significance.

He took a step forward. "I was trying to protect you, Elise. It was obvious that he was some kind of nut. He sent you these...epistles of obsessed love—"

"You read Dylan's letters?" But of course he had. How else would he know she'd met Dylan in Mexico—or what they'd experienced together?

Elise felt completely invaded. And robbed. Keith had seen the proof of Dylan's love—and she still had not. "How could you read something so personal, so private?"

"I didn't read them all," he explained hotly, as if that would mitigate the transgression. "I'm not sorry I read what I did, though. In every letter, he said he was coming back for you. It wasn't hard to convince your landlord and the authorities that it was best if you just disappeared. I returned from Oregon and asked you to marry me. When you agreed, I concluded that whoever Dylan Colman was, he definitely meant nothing to you. Why would I have left any evidence of him in those boxes if I thought he'd be a threat to us?"

"I don't know why," Elise said, momentarily puzzled by this consideration, until an explanation rose out of her consciousness. "Unless you were just so sure I would never reach the point where I'd ask these questions, would want to confront whatever heartache lay hidden in my past." She pressed her lips together to contain the regret that singed the edge of her resolve. She *was* to blame for certain things that had gone wrong—it wasn't what she'd done, but what she had not.

Apparently seeing an advantage in her silence, Keith pressed on. "When Dylan Colman showed up here a few days ago, you still didn't know him. You were *afraid* of him. You tell me, Elise. What should I have done?"

"What should you have done?" she repeated sadly. "What should we both have done from the very beginning? We should have looked for the truth, painful as it might have been. Or still might be."

"And what is the truth? Not half an hour ago you said you didn't know Dylan Colman."

Elise closed her eyes, engulfed in her remorse—at learning of Keith's complicity, and at her own culpability in this whole situation, because the question remained: *Why, still, don't I know Dylan?* It cut her as deeply as a knife thrust.

And Keith knew it did. "Tell me, Elise. Where's your mystery man now?" she heard him ask derisively, hitting his mark accurately, another razor-sharp blade sinking into her heart.

She opened her eyes. "He'll be back," she declared, as much to convince herself as Keith. "I know he will."

"Yeah, and when he does, I'll be waiting."

She heard the threat, loud and clear. Viento Blanco was this man's territory, the last bit of his life he had some control over. He meant to fight for it—for her, as long as she remained here. Well, he could have it.

This house, however, was her aunt's territory. Hers as well, such as it was. She did have a home here, a haven, someone who loved her. And she, too, would protect this place and her aunt's love for her. "Get out of this house. Now."

Another brief tussle of wills ensued. Finally, Keith turned and left. The sound of the front door slamming met their ears.

Elise sagged against the wall at her side, drained by the emotion she'd just exerted. She was under no illusion she had seen the last of him.

Again, she noticed, her headache had receded with the advent of her anger.

She glanced at her aunt, who was batting her eyes furiously in her own attempt to deal with the intensity of the past few minutes. Elise squeezed the softly rounded shoulders.

"I'm sorry you had to witness that, Aunt Char. I guess it's pretty obvious there won't be a wedding tomorrow."

Her aunt shook her head in that distracted way she had. "He went through your mail? Hid all kinds of things from you—"

"Don't worry," Elise said, interpreting the root of her aunt's distress, "if he's concealed anything from you having to do with your affairs, I promise you right now Keith Hurston will regret it for the rest of his life. And we'll find someone right away to take over your financial matters."

Charlotte seemed reassured not in the least. "I've always known Keith could be somewhat domineering, but he shouldn't have kept it from you that that . . . stranger, whoever he is, was looking for you. I don't care what his reasons were. Neither of us had any warning that he might show up." She stared up at her niece. "You must never see him again!'' Elise wondered if her aunt meant Dylan or Keith. ''Never! And if he comes back here...'' Wrinkled lips ceased their trembling and set in a resolute line. ''Sheriff Roswell's mother—God rest her soul—was one of my best friends. I'll make sure he takes care of Keith Hurston.''

So that answered Elise's question. Family was family, and Aunt Char meant to do some protecting of her own. Elise hugged her aunt tightly, never loving this sweet old woman more. She suspected she hadn't given her aunt enough credit over the past few months—or over the past seven years.

With vigor, Charlotte returned the hug before pulling away. She seemed startled to notice the compress and glass in her hands, and realized why she held them. ''You poor dear! Your head must be splitting from all this.''

''Actually—''

''We've got to get you into bed.'' She marched into Elise's room with Elise following as best she could.

''Now, you take your pill,'' Aunt Charlotte said, ''and change into a nightgown so you'll be comfortable. I'll have to redo this compress.''

''Aunt Char, wait.'' Elise shed her coat and flung it over the back of a chair. ''My head's fine for now. I need to do something else.''

''What?'' Her aunt turned and took in the gauzy red dress. Her eyes lifted to Elise's in perplexity.

''Never mind what I've got on,'' Elise said quickly, forestalling any comment. ''I need to go through the boxes in the attic. Now.''

''Now? Dearest child, I told you, you didn't have to do that. They're really no bother, honestly they aren't.''

''But there are...things in them I've got to face.'' Elise took Charlotte by her shoulders and stooped to look at her aunt with as much reassurance as she could muster, despite the impatient urgency she suddenly felt. She had no idea when or if Keith would come back—or Dylan—and she had to get to the boxes and see if whatever was in them would pique her memory.

Where *was* Dylan, Elise wondered frantically.

"W-what things?" her aunt asked, as if Pandora herself stood before her.

"Not bad things. Things that'll help me. I want to paint again, Aunt Char. I want to live a normal life again." She swallowed her fear with difficulty. She had to believe that this catharsis would be good for her. "I've got to do this," she said, as much for her own benefit as her aunt's.

"All right, dear, but you still know you don't have to do anything you don't want to."

"I want to," Elise assured her. "I need to."

They started to leave the room, heading for the attic. A man appeared in the doorway, blocking their exit. Elise and her aunt gasped as one.

"Dylan!"

Elise threw her arms around his neck. He clasped her close, the moist oilskin of his duster dampening her dress's thin material clear through to the skin. She barely noticed. He was here.

"I apologize for barging into your house uninvited," Dylan told her aunt. "I knocked, but no one seemed to hear me."

Belatedly, Elise remembered Charlotte. If her own heart had throbbed in surprise, she could imagine what her elderly aunt's was doing at this moment. She turned, still in Dylan's embrace. Her aunt stared at the both of them.

"Aunt Charlotte, I believe you may have met Dylan Colman."

Charlotte smiled uncertainly.

"I was trying to avoid being seen," he explained further. "I've a feeling I'm persona non grata in Viento Blanco right now." His eyes were dark and purposeful as they settled on the woman in his arms. "I hope only so far as Keith Hurston is concerned."

Tenderly, Elise laid her hand on his cheek. "Don't worry, Aunt Char. He's the good guy," she said, so very, very glad that he was here, especially when she needed him. She recalled her purpose. "Aunt Char, would you mind going downstairs and keeping an eye out for Keith? Dylan and I have something we must do."

Her aunt shifted on her feet, looking ready to protest and, again, protect. "I'll be fine," Elise said gently. "Trust me on this one, all right?"

"All right, Elise," her aunt answered in a muted voice. Elise hoped Charlotte was disoriented by the swiftness of the last sequence of events rather than by their upsetting nature. In any case, nothing could stop her and Dylan now. The answers were at hand.

"The attic," she explained at his questioning look, after Charlotte had departed. "Keith brought back what was left of my belongings from Oregon and stored them there. I've resisted going through them for months." She wet her lips nervously. "I think we'll find something in them that will stir my memory." She tried to evade the fear that continued to dog her and appear confident. She knew, however, that her apprehension and consequently her doubt showed.

Pinpoints of Dylan's own apprehensions pricked at the back of his black eyes. Yet he nodded firmly. "Then let's see what we can find."

She unwound her arms from his neck, but his hand on the back of her own neck stayed her movement and brought her face close to his. "Kiss me once, before we go up there," he said against her lips. "For luck."

Without hesitation, Elise raised her chin and sealed her mouth to his. Dylan dragged her against his chest with critical urgency. Trepidation fueled their sudden passion, desperation for and against each other twining as did their tongues. Their bodies pressed closer for fear of not getting close enough. Whatever they had yet to discover about each other, about themselves, it mustn't come between them. And yet the nature and timing of this kiss brought home the reality that it very well could.

Whatever happened, she was so glad he was here to go through this with her.

They broke apart suddenly, knowing it was now or never. Dylan gripped her hand in his, and they walked down the narrow hall to the door at the end of it.

Elise found the door opened with none of the resistance she'd felt the last time she'd taken the porcelain knob in her hand. She closed the door behind them, locking it without thinking. Her eyes met Dylan's. Had she done so to add another impediment to her again running away from whatever lay at the top of the stairs?

Not this time. Not with Dylan.

The steps creaked under their feet. From the roof's ridgepole, the rafters slanted downward at a severe angle, almost to the wooden floor. Thin light drifted in from four dormer windows on the west side. The smell was almost sweet—dust and damp wood and things whose usefulness were outlived. In the middle of the floor stood a crowd of boxes as if they'd been hastily dumped there without even a thought of assimilating them into the neat organization surrounding them.

It was cold in the attic, and Elise shivered. Without a word, Dylan removed his coat and draped it around her shoulders. She knelt in front of the boxes. He dropped to his knees beside her.

With a deep breath Elise tore open the first box, as if a canned snake would pop from it. Nothing there but kitchen items: silverware, measuring cups, pot holders. Still, she pawed through the contents, all familiar to her. A sense of nostalgia crept through her, a yearning to be surrounded by her things once again.

But no memory.

She glanced up at Dylan, who'd remained immobile during her search. She shook her head and went on to the next box. And the next.

The first article of singularity she found was the red dress. It was folded, still on its hanger and protected within a dry-cleaning sleeve, among other clothes. Elise pulled it out of the plastic and held it up. As Dylan had mentioned, it was nearly the same as the one she had on. She ran her hand over the crushed material, trying to empty her mind so that it could be filled with the memories of this dress. Nothing came to her, but then she realized it might be because the dress she wore right now—the recent recollection of how he'd given it to her and what had transpired after he had— was keeping her from focusing on the garment she held in her hands.

After several minutes in which she stared so hard the red became a blur before her eyes, Elise looked up. Dylan's brows rose in question. Again she shook her head, afraid her voice would reveal her growing disappointment.

Then she found her art supplies. A pigment-stained palette, pencils and charcoal rubber-banded together. Suddenly tense, she lifted out a gray metal tackle box-type case and set it aside for the moment. At the bottom of the cardboard box was a commercial sketch pad with the edge of a sheet of paper sticking out from it. Slowly, she open the cover and found . . . Dylan.

There were two sketches of him, one done in ink on a piece of hotel stationery—Casa de Miguel, Puerto Vallarta—the other was a charcoal done on the thicker paper of the sketch pad. Elise stared at the two renderings. They were the same, not similar but exactly the same as the one in her desk downstairs that she'd been unable to finish. Yet both of these were completed, and she saw how it truly had been with her and Dylan. He wasn't smiling, yet the whole of his countenance radiated happiness. The way that the mouth was drawn—masculine lips bowed sensuously—along with the intensity in his eyes . . . Here was a man very much in love.

With infinite care, she set the sketches aside, eager now to build on this discovery. She flipped open the lid of the tackle box. Everything lay in neat rows in their plastic compartments, just as she remembered leaving them.

Hands shaking, Elise picked up and examined each brush, each tube of paint. Her heart filled as the feel of them produced not dread but longing. God, how she'd missed her painting! She swept the baby-soft bristles of one brush across her palm and it was indeed like touching a beloved babe, the sweetest of newborn life. She reached into the case, impatient to experience more of this feeling. Her fingers touched something unfamiliar, and she froze.

"What is it, Elise?" Dylan asked quickly.

She didn't answer, just pulled out a thin stack of letters tied with a ribbon. "Your letters," she said almost inaudibly. "To me." Questions rose to her lips like bubbles of air seeking escape, and Elise turned her head to look at him, causing his coat to slip off one of her shoulders. Black eyes impenetrable, he tugged the coat back up to cover her. His hand remained on her shoulder, his arm across her back. He was here, he would support her, but she must find the answers to her questions herself.

Her gaze shifted to the sketches. "He hasn't seen these," she said.

"Hurston?"

"Yes. Something tells me he hasn't seen the sketches or these letters." Her gaze fell and blurred as she contemplated the bundle of envelopes, lovingly secured, and she was profoundly grateful. "So I do have a piece of my past that hasn't been exposed to prying eyes. A piece of you that's all mine."

"Read them, Elise," Dylan commanded softly.

With a catch in her breathing, she slid a letter from its envelope.

Dear Ellie—

It doesn't seem like it was only hours ago we left each other. I miss you already. That's why I'm writing this— besides the fact I've got another ten hours on planes until I reach Saudi. I'm glad to be starting this assignment, mainly because it'll mean I can come back to you all the more quickly. It should be interesting, though. I'll be busy...

I guess it's pretty evident that nothing new has happened in the few hours since I saw you. But all I can think about is you...you...you. Ways I can bring you closer to me, make the longing less. I keep thinking about the last night we spent together, when I held you and caressed you . . .

The words were intensely intimate, incredibly evocative, sending a bittersweet ache to burrow deep into the center of her abdomen. So she had the answer to that question, as well. They *were* lovers.

Elise leaned back against Dylan's chest as his arms surrounded her, his steady breathing gently rocking her, and both of them read on, read all the letters. Keith was right; to the uninformed, the person revealed on the pages might seem obsessed. To Elise, though, knowing Dylan, they communicated all the yearning of the man in the sketches, the one who was deeply in love. With her.

She had proof, then, of his presence in her life. And still she didn't remember him. Yes, she believed, but she did not remember.

How could she tell him? How had they failed each other so grievously that she couldn't remember him, even now?

Tucking her chin against her chest to avoid Dylan's scrutiny, Elise said nothing for several minutes as she fought the despair stealing up on her. How foolish she'd been, pinning her hopes on a few cardboard crates! She'd done it again, looked for answers in something or someone who would never, could never provide them. And now to discover that the sum of her life's possessions had no ability to bring that life back to her . . .

What had she so greatly dreaded here? Seeing and touching her paints and brushes hadn't produced the aversion she'd feared it would. Reading Dylan's letters left her regretful, not frightened. Or was the key now that she was not facing any of these truths alone?

Indeed, the empathy she felt from him was almost tangible, and her own sense of compassion rose up in her. Dylan had been hoping, too, wanting as acutely as she to know what it was that kept her from remembering him. Because whatever it was, no matter the extent of their love for each other, it remained a separating force between them, as surely as persisted the gulf between the present and her past.

Yet for brief instances they'd bridged that gap or seemed to, each time he'd held her and kissed her. The connection had flowed between them, stayed her doubts and reinforced her conviction.

Elise lifted her chin, though she still didn't turn her head and meet his eyes. "I believe you now, Dylan," she said. "Everything you said we did or were—*are*—to each other."

"But do you remember, Ellie?" he asked quietly.

At his question, she hesitated involuntarily in her removal of his coat from around her shoulders. Then, with purpose, she spread it beside her on the rough wood floor. She turned to him.

"What matters right now is that we love each other," she said, not answering his question. She clasped her hands behind his neck and tugged him toward her as she leaned back. He resisted for a split second before he was forced to support them both with one arm around her and the other locked at the elbow, fingers splayed against the horizontal surface. Gravity, at least, was on her side, and he continued to lower her until her back touched the smooth oilskin and he lay full-length on top of her, a thousand questions in his eyes.

Dylan propped himself up on his elbows, holding himself away from her, but Elise was dogged in maintaining as much physical contact between them as possible with the twining of her arms around his neck. "What's going on here, Elise?" he asked, his voice low and rough with the passion she'd already ignited within him.

"I love you, Dylan," she explained, gliding her lips across his rugged jawline. "I want to be close to you." She found his earlobe and caressed it with her tongue. "As close as I can be."

His breathing was ragged in her ear. "Do you remember, then?" he whispered.

Elise heard the hope in his voice, and again tears stung. She swallowed them back. She couldn't lie to him. "Whenever I've felt the beginning of a connection to you, I've been in your arms. That's when the thread of remembrance is strongest." She brought his face up so she could see his eyes. "Make love to me, Dylan. And maybe the connection will complete itself."

She saw what her words did to him as his dark eyes grew darker. Yet the questions remained there, as well. "It's wrong, Ellie, to use each other this way. You must know that."

"But what choice have we?" she pressed. He wouldn't fight her, would he? "Nothing else has worked!" With effort, she moderated her tone, her look. "Where's the harm? We've been lovers before."

"It could hurt you, Elise." His features twisted. "*I've* hurt you. Somehow, I've damaged your trust—"

"It doesn't matter." She reached for his hand—and placed it over her breast. He immediately stiffened, but she held his palm against her. "I'm promising you, it doesn't matter what you've done."

"It doesn't make it right," he rasped.

She stifled further objection with her mouth over his. He held back at first, then something seemed to unleash itself within him and he pressed her back against the hard floor, his mouth seeking the depths of hers. His fingers closed over her flesh.

Elise strained toward him as ardently, wanting to fill her mind, soul, heart and body with this man and his powerful energy. He could make her believe anything, *had* made her believe. And it was his own desperate need to believe that brought him to her.

"Make it happen," she demanded between kisses. "Just as it did that last night together."

His fingers gripped her bare shoulder, then slackened to drift over her collarbone and throat. Then back toward her shoulder again, down her upper arm, taking the shirred elastic sleeve with them. And exposing her to his hot breath.

Elise moaned, transfixed by his touch. She wanted to touch him, too. She pulled his shirt from his waistband and sighed when her hands experienced the warm, hard feel of his back, his murmur of pleasure. Neither was his hand idle as he slid it down her thigh and inched her skirt upward until he met nylon-covered skin, her silky hosiery a stimulation-enhancing texture between them.

Dylan plunged his face into the crook of her neck on a groan of desire and frustration. And reservation.

"Tell me," he said against her throat, "before we go any further."

"What?"

"Do you remember anything? Anything at all?"

She groaned her own frustration. "No! It doesn't matter, don't you see? It doesn't matter what you did, what I did."

"Maybe it doesn't now," he said, his lips brushing almost in consolation against the mole on her nape. *The one just like her mother's.* "But it will."

Another denial sprang to her lips. It died before she'd voiced it. He was right. *What had happened?* The question rang in her head like a challenge. At last, she was ready to take on the answer, because she truly did believe that whatever the truth was, it could not be as bad as this endless not knowing.

I want to know the truth!

The pain hit like a wrecker's ball against the side of her head. In reaction, Elise sucked in a lungful of air, then clutched Dylan to her, hoping he would think she'd gasped in passion rather than distress. He must have detected something amiss anyway, for he tried to retreat from her. She held him fast.

Elise fought to block out the crushing pressure, but it would have been like trying to ignore a stake being driven into her brain. Despite her determination that it not stop her, the next wave of pain made her body go rigid.

"Elise!" Dylan pulled away from her. She grabbed fistfuls of his shirtfront.

"Don't stop, Dylan," she pleaded through clenched teeth, gulping down her nausea. She knew she should have taken two of those damnable pills! "We're close...so close."

"Is it your head?"

"It's...nothing." The pain was a battering ram in its forcefulness.

She opened her eyes to find him, encourage him—but her vision had narrowed. What she had left were pulsing spots of nothing. Elise swallowed back panic, remembered that anger helped. "No," she grated, speaking to her pain as if it were a living thing, "don't do this to me. I need more...time. Leave me alone!"

A torturous spasm racked her and she cried out.

She felt herself being lifted, duster and all, and tucked into strong arms. Heavy but rapid steps told her she was being taken from the attic, rushed down the hall and laid on her bed. Swift fingers adjusted her dress even as she heard Dylan's shout, "Charlotte, come quickly!"

And the pain went on and on.

"What is it?" From faraway she heard her aunt's voice, alarm in its tone.

"She needs a doctor," Dylan answered.

"No!" Elise pushed herself up on her elbows. The room careened sideways. "Don't call Dr. Emerson! Not yet. I've got to...push harder." She lifted her gaze and found Dylan at the end of the tunnel, his face ravaged with her pain, but also with a torture all his own. "Please, Dylan. We're getting closer to the truth. That's why my head hurts so badly." She fell back on the pillow as another constriction wrenched her. "We can't stop now.... Push...harder."

"To hell with pushing! This is madness, Elise. We've got to get you to a doctor."

"The pills," she stalled. A wave of pain made her bite down on her lip until she tasted blood. She forced her eyes open and tried to focus on her aunt as she haunted the doorway. "I've got pills for the headaches. In the bathroom."

In what seemed like bare seconds, her fists were pried open and a glass pressed against one palm, a tablet to the other. The pill grew bitter on her tongue as she tried several times to wash it down. Finally she did, but she was not at all certain it wouldn't come right back up again.

The room was silent for several minutes while Elise fought the headache, gripping Dylan's hand as he sat beside her. But it was no use. The pain had dug in for the duration. Tears of despair ran down her temples into her hair.

"Will you let me call the doctor now?" Dylan finally asked. She could tell the wait had cost him.

"What good would it do?" she asked weakly. "The headache's not going away. Nothing will make it go away except finding out the truth."

"It's pretty clear what the truth is," he said, his hand soothing back her hair with extraordinary tenderness. "I've hurt you, Elise, and it's something your heart can't forgive me for, even if your mind has. And you're going to go on hurting as long as I remain here."

Even through a muddle of misery, Elise caught his meaning. Genuine panic leapt up in her. "No!" She caught his hand in a death grip. "You're not leaving me."

"I can't do this to you, Ellie."

"You can't leave me now!" Her voice was shrill, near hysteria.

He gathered her to him, holding her as if, indeed, he would never leave, never let her go. "The pain is killing you."

"It'll kill me if you leave!" She clung to him, and for a few short minutes Dylan cleaved to her, his cheek pressed hard to the crown of her head, his strong arms bands of steel that, rather than imprisoning her, had always made her feel more free.

"What can I do?" he asked, though it seemed he wasn't speaking to her. "After talking to those doctors, I thought I'd found the answer, but what do they know about you, about me? Am I kidding myself—and you—because I can't face the truth myself?'' He tucked her more firmly against his chest. "Who else might know...?"

At last he set her away from him. Disoriented by her head splitting in two, she didn't register at first the coolness around her where there had been warmth moments before. She felt a touch as light as a feather on her cheek. Then nothing.

Elise forced her eyes open. The room spun crazily. She picked out her desk on one rotation, the door to her closet the next, then Aunt Char standing near the doorway to the hall. But no one else.

"Dylan!" she screamed. Frantically, Elise scrambled off the bed—and crashed to the floor as dizziness flowed and ebbed in her. On her hands and knees, she panted, drawing a measure of strength. Shaking off her aunt's hold on her arm, she clutched the bedpost and dragged herself upright.

What had he said? She tried to relive the past few moments when he'd held her. *What had he said?* Nowhere, though, in her agonized brain did she find the words she needed. He'd always told her he'd come back—except this time.

Anger helps. "Damn you, Dylan Colman," she ground out. "You can't do this to me. I won't let you." Pain plunged into her brain with the force of a guillotine, its bite clean and sharp and deep. "I don't deserve it! I didn't do anything... *How can you leave me when I need you most?*"

On her cry, Elise found herself immersed in a memory.

Chapter Nine

Rain poured down in sheets, the road was slick and winding as it curved around a jagged coast. All was dark but the patch of pavement illuminated by her headlights.

She should stop. At the next turnoff she would. The grade of the road grew steeper, and she found herself constantly riding the brake. Why was she out on a night like this, anyway?

A turnoff! It had come up on her quickly, though, and she slammed on the brakes—too hard. The car fishtailed before going into a skid. Remembering her high school drivers' Ed, Elise cranked the wheel the other way, steering into the skid, but she was unfamiliar with the car and the road. She headed straight for the dull gray highway barrier. Straight for the cliff.

She spun the steering wheel again, averting the danger of the cliff. The car wove the other way. She watched helplessly through the windshield as the embankment rushed forward to meet her. And she knew she would crash, and crash hard. She turned her head to the side, raised her arms to protect herself, but nothing would stop the inevitable.

Everything took on a strange torpidity even as her mind raced to react. Her life flashed before her: childhood, adolescence. Losing her parents. Understanding sank in. This was what they had gone through. The sheer terror, the helplessness, the anguish in knowing your time on this earth was up and who you would be leaving behind. She knew then they hadn't wanted to leave her. They loved her!

Elise collapsed onto her bed as her tortured mind relived the bang and screech of metal on rock, metal on metal. The way the world had turned on end as her car flipped over. And over. The sickly give of bones and living tissue. The sharp crack of the side of her skull against the roof. And the pain, *the pain!*

She was trapped in steaming wreckage. Had Mom and Dad hurt like this? Something warm dripped into her eyes. Hearing the grinding of bone against bone, mingling with the sound of someone moaning, she understood how such pain could wring the heart and soul out of a person. What on earth could be worth such suffering? Certainly not...her. No, Elise couldn't have asked her parents to suffer like this, not even for her. Yet hazy intuition told her they had suffered, terribly. It nearly undid her, realizing what they must have endured in those moments before death claimed them.

Oh, Mom...Dad... Her heart, in that moment, broke into a thousand tiny pieces.

An ominous hissing came from behind her. Through her confusion, Elise smelled gas. She'd have to get out of there soon, very soon. That would mean trying to move. She didn't think she could do it. It would be so much easier to give up the ghost.

But for some reason, she didn't want to die. She wanted to live!

She drifted in an all-encompassing blackness. A complete and total aloneness. She *was* alive, but barely. She tried to reach out, touch something real within this darkness, but she was too weak. Too weary. The pain...it wasn't worth it, all this pain.

Yes, it is. You must try—for Dylan. This was why she was still alive. He couldn't go through what she had, losing someone she loved. And he did love her. The knowledge stimulated her. She had to try for him. She deserved a chance, didn't she, to make a life with him?

Of course, she did. So she'd come back—for him.

Elise remembered, then, floating in and out of wakefulness, everything impressions rather than solid reality. Somehow she knew she was surrounded by strangers. No one knew her name. And why was she trussed up tighter than a Thanksgiving turkey? She felt trapped again within the wreckage. She fought against the strictures with whatever feeble strength she could muster and earned vague admonishments.

She stopped fighting. All right, then. He'd come to her. He'd promised he would.

Aeons of time passed, and still she waited. But reality was intruding. Through slitted lids, she found glaring hospital white enveloped her. She squeezed her eyes shut to hide from it. She heard voices. None of them was Dylan's.

She was returning to consciousness—and Dylan wasn't there. She'd come back for him—yet there was no Dylan.

And so... there was no Dylan.

Elise's eyes shot open. She remembered. *She remembered!* Then her eyes filled with tears, for she knew why she'd forgotten him.

Her headache was gone, but in its place was poignant understanding.

"Aunt Char," she said brokenly.

"I'm here, child." A warm soft hand found hers. Elise held on for dear life as returning images marched in an unrelenting procession across her mind.

"I was... driving down to see you," Elise explained haltingly, her eyes shut to absorb the details of her awakening memory. "I'd met a man... in Mexico."

"Dylan?" her aunt asked.

She nodded. "I had gone there to think, to make a... fresh start."

"In what?"

"My—my life," she said, her voice gathering strength as she did. "I knew that ever since Mom and Dad died I'd been hiding from the world, trying to keep inside all the emotions about their deaths that I still hadn't handled. I thought that I was finally ready to deal with them, I just didn't know how. But I was scared, too. I didn't think it was going to be easy to purge such deep emotions. So I took a trip, hoping a complete change of scenery would clear my mind." Elise gave a shuddering sigh. "Or maybe leaving was still a form of avoidance."

Yet she *had* wanted to be well; she'd actively sought out the ways to be whole again. She'd been willing to face the pain, even before...

"Then I met Dylan." Elise saw him as clearly as if he stood before her. "I'd never known anyone like him. Meeting him... it *was* like a lightning bolt. Or fate. For two weeks, we were inseparable." She saw it all. They had sailed, walked the beaches hand in hand, and loved the nights away. "But I knew even then I couldn't commit to him the way he wanted me to without first taking care of the emotional problems I'd come to Mexico to sort out. So I returned to Oregon, and thought some more. His letters came, nearly every day." Elise swallowed back a fresh onslaught of tears. "I missed him terribly, Aunt Char."

"I'm sure you did, dear," Charlotte murmured with a tender squeeze of her fingers.

"Finally I couldn't stand to be apart from him any longer. I knew the restrictions of his job. We'd have to marry to be together. But before I could do that, I still needed to take care of those feelings bottled up inside of me—anger, grief, mistrust—purge them with the one person in this world who'd experienced some of the same emotions." She opened her eyes and looked at her aunt. "You, Aunt Char. I needed to be with you."

Tears swam in the old woman's blue eyes and spilled over. "I wanted to reach out to you, child, so many times in the past seven years. But you were always so composed, like nothing bothered you. Like you didn't need my help."

Elise saw her aunt's throat worked spasmodically as Charlotte tried, even now, to control tender emotions, lest they be met with indifference. And Elise wished to return to a different time in her past, when a seventeen-year-old girl had shut out the world, including this dear woman.

"I knew you had to be suffering," her aunt continued, "but I didn't know how to handle you, what to say. So I didn't do anything. And I'm so very sorry for that, Elise."

Elise sat up and engulfed her aunt in a powerful hug. "I don't blame you, Aunt Char. I must have been impossible to understand. I didn't want anything from anyone—pity, sympathy. I held everything inside, I guess because I thought that if I vented my grief, you'd see how needy I was and think me a burden."

"Never," her aunt pressed her wet cheek against Elise's, "I would never think you a burden."

"But I did. Why else would Mom and Dad have left me? I couldn't bear having anyone else feel that way about me— because then I'd have to face the possibility that they would abandon me, too, just like Mom and Dad had seemed to."

Yes, it was all clear to her now, and tears of relief sped down her cheeks, mingling with her aunt's. Her parents hadn't abused her, but she had held them responsible for a transgression they had no control over: dying.

Elise and Charlotte held each other, and at last they mourned. On a stormy night seven years ago, two loved ones had been taken from them both. No one had been to blame, not the man and woman who'd died, least of all the two women they left behind.

As Dylan had left her, Elise thought. As she'd left him.

I didn't mean to! I didn't mean to hurt you. Neither of them had, yet the damage on both sides had been very real. What must he be thinking right now? He'd left her side because it hurt her for him to stay—and deserting her killed him inside. He couldn't go on thinking for one minute longer that his presence in her life caused her any sort of pain.

Elise pulled away from Charlotte, grasping the liver-spotted hands in hers. "I've got to find him."

"Dylan?" her aunt asked. "Child, are you sure you're up to this?"

"My headache's gone—I think for good." Elise's mind raced. He must have gone back to Healdsburg. "Aunt Char, quickly. Call information and get the number for the Pine Cone Inn, then call there. Ask for Dylan Colman's room. I'm going to change."

Her aunt scuttled out of the room while Elise slid the red dress off. Tenderly, she draped it over the back of a chair. Then she pulled on warm slacks and a sweater. By the time she'd donned a pair of sturdy shoes and hurried down the stairs, Charlotte had the inn on the phone.

"They say there's no one there," she told Elise, who took the receiver.

"Do you have any idea when he's coming back?" she asked, knowing the question was ridiculous. This wasn't a first-class hotel.

"No, miss."

A horrible possibility struck her. "He hasn't checked out, has he?"

"No, miss. Is there any message?"

"Yes. The message is to stay there. I'm—tell him Elise is coming. And he should call here—" she rattled off her aunt's number "—when he gets in. This is very important, understand?"

"Yes, miss."

Elise replaced the receiver and turned to her aunt. "If Dylan calls, tell him what happened, that I *remember*. That everything's all right. I'm going to look for him in case he hasn't gone back to Healdsburg."

"But Elise..." Aunt Charlotte stood rooted beside the phone as her niece, who not ten minutes ago had lain on her bed incapacitated by pain, made a dash for the door.

"What, Aunt Char?" Elise asked impatiently as she grabbed a key ring from its hook and whirled to face her aunt.

Then she knew the source of Charlotte's hesitation. Both of them stared at the keys in her hand.

Charlotte was already bustling forward. "I'll go look for Dylan," she said, reaching for her coat.

"Someone has to stay here in case he calls—or comes back."

"Then you stay. I'll go."

"No," Elise said faintly, then with more conviction, "no. I need to search for him myself."

"But what if you get one of those anxiety attacks? It's too dangerous."

"I haven't completely lost my driving skills. And it's broad daylight outside." They peered out the backdoor window and beheld the dullest of views, hardly encouraging. Perhaps she *should* stay here and wait for him. Dylan was sure to come back sometime. Or would he? He believed he hurt her by staying, but that didn't mean he'd go for good, did it? Elise recalled that he'd said his time here was nearly up. Would he go back to Saudi without seeing her again? He couldn't!

"I've got to go myself, Aunt Char." Even as she repeated the words, a latent response returned to her. She had lain trapped in a maze of twisted metal, divested of hope and nearly of her lifeblood. And so alone.

Never again. She'd never again put herself into such a position of vulnerability. In a car or in her life. Subconsciously she'd made that promise to herself, and it had started the avalanche of events that had swept away her memory and made her pledge herself to a man who never even had a chance of touching her heart.

Even understanding what she was feeling, and why, did not relieve Elise's fear. Her apprehensions escalated as she stood staring at the keys in her hand. Apparently her memory was not completely restored, for another recollection returned to her: Just as she'd projected herself into her parents' minds at the moment of impact, she'd somehow left her own body and she saw herself in the minutes directly after her own crash. Strangely detached from the scene below, she had floated above the ground, observing the unfortunate young woman who lay draped over the steering wheel, vapor swirling around her. And Elise knew then how close she'd come to dying. How she'd wanted to die. Yet something had pulled her back, and it had been the love of a very special man.

Her fingers closed over the cold metal car keys. "I'm going," she told her aunt.

"But Elise—"

"And I promise—I'll be back."

Elise stood on the back step for a moment, peering into the mist, hoping for one moment that Dylan had not left and perhaps waited in the shadows for her. Yet even in the limiting gloom, she could see she was alone. She would have to go to him this time.

She marched on not completely steady legs to her aunt's car, unlocked the door and slid into the front seat before she had a chance to think any longer about what she was doing. She inserted the key in the ignition and turned. The engine immediately came to life. Jerking the gearshift into Reverse, she backed out of the driveway and into the street. Then she paused for a moment, fastening her seat belt, adjusting the rearview mirror. The fog was as thick behind the car as in front of it. She had no excuse not to go forward.

This damnable fog! It was always there, surrounding her, closing her in, trapping her in a nebulous snare. Had it been the least bit more substantial, she could have fought it. But it would never go away, not as long as she remained in Viento Blanco. The only way out of the pervasive mist was to push through it, refuse to let it get in the way of what she wanted. And she wanted to find Dylan. She had to find him.

Elise took a deep breath. Fear and anxiety were still on her shoulder, making her stomach churn and causing a tremor in her hands despite her efforts to quell it. Likely, it

would always be this way when she got behind the wheel of
a car; she shouldn't expect complete calm and composure.
But, Elise decided, she could expect to control her phobia
enough so that she could proceed with her life in a normal
manner. That seemed a more reasonable goal.

She tugged the lever on the steering column into Drive and
decreased pressure on the brake. The car advanced an inch.
Then another inch. Soon she had reached the end of the
street and had turned the corner.

No headache. She'd feared that most of all. The victory
inspired her.

She noted with a nervous chuckle that she was doing a
rubber-burning five miles per hour. Her foot left the brake
pedal and gave the car some gas. It accelerated steadily until she was going twenty-five. She glanced up from the patch
of road directly in front of the bumper and saw that she was
heading for Seaspray Avenue.

Hope such as she hadn't felt in months buoyed her. She
would find Dylan.

Two hours later Elise's optimism was showing a little
tarnish around the edges. She'd crisscrossed Viento Blanco,
even made the trip down to the marina on an insubstantial
hunch that Dylan might have gone there to seek solace in
one of the activities he liked best. Yet deep down she knew
he wouldn't go out for a sail on a day like this. The bay was
socked in.

Finally she'd taken the highway out of town. Toward
Healdsburg.

Dylan had not returned to the Pine Cone Inn, either. She
sat in the Pontiac near the entrance, with a clear view of
every car that came and went in the parking lot. But no Dylan.

Where had he gone? The clerk said he hadn't checked out,
so he must be planning to come back. She held on to that
detail as if it were a lifeline. He wouldn't leave the country
without coming back here. But when he'd left her he'd been

as distressed as she'd been. As disheartened and bereft of hope.

Maybe he'd stopped for something to eat. She glanced at her watch. Four o'clock. Surely he'd have returned by now.

It helped to plan. Even if she found him and explained, Elise realized, they would still have to get married in order for her to join him overseas. There were probably all sorts of details to work out: passports and visas—would inoculations be required? All of these required weeks of turnaround. It might be more feasible for him to finish his assignment and come back for her then.

Her fingers locked around the steering wheel. She wouldn't let him! She couldn't let him go again, not this time. She'd follow him to the ends of the earth if she had to.

Elise tried for calm, deliberately loosening her fingers. His superiors might give him a few more weeks of leave. Yet Dylan had made it very clear he was on borrowed time right now, as it was. His job and reputation were important to him. Even with the exigency of their situation, she couldn't ask that of him. He'd never ask her to put her art aside for him...

Elise studied the passing traffic without really seeing it. In a way, she *had* given up her art for Dylan—that was why she hadn't been able to paint these past months. In the recesses of her healing brain, she must have told herself that was what it would take to bring him back to her. But why?

Because her father's job had taken her parents from her.

Dormant anger and resentment crept up on her, and she understood. Her father hadn't needed to make the house call that night; her mother hadn't needed to go with him. Elise realized now how angry she'd been, angry at both her parents for what she'd perceived as their carelessness and desertion, which had seemed much too deliberate. But she'd bottled all this inside of her, where it had had seven years to churn and build pressure.

Then she'd had her accident and connected it to her mother and father's accident. The two separate but similar events must have commingled in her mind. When she'd awakened from her coma, alive, she must have figured that had they also really wanted to live, they could have. So she blocked out the part of her life in which she'd begun to forgive her parents—and blocked out Dylan, too, the person who'd abandoned her for his work as they had.

You just weren't there.

Dylan had known or at least suspected that was the cause of her memory lapse. He'd always made it a point to tell her he'd be back. She had to believe one more time that he truly meant it. Of course she was no psychiatrist; she was guessing herself. Yet it made sense. The lethargy, the inability to concentrate, the aversion to returning to her vocation. She never knew she was blocking anything out, but she'd known she wasn't getting well. No one had known...except Keith.

Who else might know? Dylan had asked just before he left her.

Foreboding sliced through her. Elise started the car and pulled out into the traffic, heading back to Viento Blanco.

Elise stopped at the curb with a telling screech of tires. She'd barely shut off the car before she was out of the driver's seat, the door slamming behind her. In a flash, she'd crossed the sidewalk to a quaint office and pushed the door open with like force.

"Where is he?" Elise demanded of the startled secretary sitting at her desk. With effort, she moderated her tone. "Lisa, I'm looking for Keith. He's not at his Santa Rosa office, is he?"

"No, Elise. He was working out of this office today, although he left just before noon."

"Has he been back? Called?"

"No..." The young woman was obviously disconcerted by her boss's fiancée barging into his office the day before their wedding and asking suspicious questions. "I thought he was with you, taking care of last-minute details like the marriage license or something."

"We're *not* getting married," Elise automatically responded, thinking irrelevantly that she and Keith had gotten their marriage license in Santa Rosa last week. It occurred to her how narrowly she'd avoided real disaster. If Dylan had come back a mere four days later, she'd have been married to Keith Hurston. With a shiver, she imagined the difficult scene that would have ensued—much worse than the one in the gallery the first day Dylan appeared. If Keith had been possessive of her then, it didn't bear thinking what he'd have done once he deemed her truly his. He'd make good on his threats, and probably with good reason.

She knew where Keith was.

Elise left the office and ran the hundred yards down the street to the police station, still hoping against hope that he'd come to his senses and hadn't acted so drastically. Her heart sank when she entered the station and found him sitting across from Frank Roswell in the sheriff's office. Then she got angry. This was the last straw.

"Where is he?" Elise demanded for the second time in five minutes. She meant Dylan, though, and Keith knew it. He stood slowly, his expression uncompromising. *"Where is he?"* she shouted.

Keith shot a quick glance at the sheriff, who was looking puzzled by the fierce woman who braced her hands on the edge of his desk and thrust her face inches from his. "If you've arrested him on no other authority than Keith Hurston's, I'll see that charges are brought against both of you."

She felt a touch on her arm that made her skin crawl. "Now, Elise," Keith said, "you're getting hysterical again—"

"No!" Elise flung off his hand, facing him. "I'm furious! And you're the one who's sick, not me. I would have let this whole matter pass, Keith, if you'd just shown the least sign of reason. But you've got this need to control that's ruining your life. I refuse to let you ruin mine. Now tell me where Dylan is."

Incredibly, he seemed about to dissemble—again! Something in her expression apparently dissuaded him, though. "He's not here," Keith answered.

She believed him, but she knew him well enough by now to know he was hiding something. Elise caught the sheriff's hesitation out of the corner of her eye. "Is that true?" she asked him.

"Well, yes, but we've just received a call from one of our patrol cars—"

The sound of someone entering the main station room met their ears. All three left Roswell's office as Dylan came around a corner. Police officers on either side of him manacled his arms with their hands. Elise made a low sound of disbelief when she saw that his hands were hidden behind him, and guessed his wrists were shackled with a pair of handcuffs. She met Dylan's gaze and saw his anger—and pain, at having her see him like this, with his own control over his life taken from him. She spun to confront Roswell.

"There's absolutely no reason to restrain him using such methods," she charged. No reason to humiliate him so.

"Ms. Nash, we have cause to believe this man could be dangerous," the sheriff defended himself. "Keith has stated that Dylan Colman assaulted you three days ago in Hurston Gallery, and that Mr. Hurston and the suspect exchanged words that nearly led to this man assaulting Mr. Hurston as well."

"He didn't assault me!"

"He did put up a struggle, ma'am," one of the officers told her, then addressed Keith and the sheriff. "We apprehended him outside the Nash home. He came back there, just like you said he would, Mr. Hurston."

Keith nodded with satisfaction as he looked at her. She realized it was her word against Keith's, and this was his territory. He'd made it clear that in this town he ruled. "Surely you see that you've gone too far with your little power games. You can't play with people's lives like this."

"I'm trying to protect you—"

"You're trying to control me, like you've tried to continue controlling Sharon! That's why she left you, isn't it?"

"And why did you leave *him?*" His face blotchy with his own anger, Keith pointed at Dylan. "Tell me that, Elise! What did he do to you, or do you still not remember him?"

Yes, I remember! She had the answer, the right answer, this time. Elise opened her mouth to respond when her gaze met Dylan's and locked, and she spied again the torture he was going through. It didn't matter what Keith Hurston believed. What mattered was that Dylan had come back. They were together again—or would be once she got him out of there.

She turned and found Keith watching the exchange of glances between them. "I guess I do owe you some credit, Keith," she said and paused a beat, observing his reaction of uncertainty before finishing her sentence, "for finding Dylan for me. Now let him go."

Again, there was a battle of wills, a tug of war, a clashing of two opposing forces as Elise's eyes riveted on the bearlike man standing next to Frank Roswell. "If you're interested in doing your job today, Sheriff," she added softly, her gaze never leaving Keith's, "you can start by arresting Keith Hurston for obstructing the delivery of the United States mail. Or should I take this matter to the federal authorities in Santa Rosa, and fill them in on some of the activities of Viento Blanco's police department while I'm there?"

At that moment the station door swept open and Charlotte Nash sailed through the doorway like a battleship at full speed, with Dr. Emerson close behind her. What was her doctor doing here? Elise wondered briefly before her attention was diverted by her aunt's voice, strident with indignation.

"Frank Roswell!" Charlotte marched up to the sheriff, her mouth trembling as Elise had seen it do hundreds of times before. This time, she realized, Aunt Char was trembling with rage. "I have never in my life encountered such a disgraceful display of brute force as I did today in front of my very home. This innocent man," she threw Dylan a compassionate and somewhat theatrical glance, "a *guest* of my niece, was dragged from his car and manhandled like a common criminal! It was the most appalling scene I've ever witnessed! If this is how Viento Blanco's law-enforcement officials conduct themselves, well, then . . ." She faltered, apparently at a loss to outline the sort of action one took in such a situation. Her considerable bosom heaved. "I do know your sainted mother wouldn't be very proud of her son today!"

The sheriff looked appropriately discomfited. He cast a glance at Keith, who himself appeared disconcerted by the sequence of events. Charlotte Nash had been a citizen of Viento Blanco for seventy years. No one in town would question her word, and if she said an injustice had taken place today, then it had.

"I'll start an investigation immediately," the sheriff told Elise.

"I could be persuaded to drop the charges," she said, facing Keith one last time, "if I were to get back all of my letters. And Dylan Colman goes free."

Amazingly—sadly—Keith looked about to argue. Then his mouth tightened and he nodded once. "You'll have the letters by nightfall."

One of the officers unlocked the handcuffs and Dylan rubbed his wrists, his black eyes on Keith. The two men stared at each other with loathing.

"Get out of here," Keith snarled.

"Gladly." Dylan held out his hand to Elise and she walked forward and took it. "And *you,*" he turned back to Keith, "get some professional help."

Elise glanced down at their twined hands and noticed the glint of blue on her finger. She tugged off Keith's ring.

"Keep it," he said, when he saw what she was doing.

And she saw what he was doing. To the bitter end. "Like hell I will," she said, tossing the ring. It sailed through the air and struck Keith in the chest before dropping with a *ching* to the floor and skittering under a desk.

Together, with Charlotte and Dr. Emerson following, Elise and Dylan exited the station, and Elise felt she was leaving behind a part of her past she knew she'd never forget, for she'd learned a lesson that would stand her in good stead the rest of her life: She must face whatever pain life brought her, confront her fears and deal with them before they controlled her. It was the only way she would ever have the kind of happiness she deserved.

Outside on the sidewalk Elise turned to her doctor, who had said nothing during the entire scene in the police station, although Elise saw that Dr. Emerson's lips were turned up in an approving smile. "I don't know why you're here, Dr. Emerson, but I'm sure glad you are. You'll never guess what happened."

"Oh, I think I can make a good try," the doctor answered, "but only because I heard some of the details from this gentleman. You've got one persistent young man here, Elise. And persuasive."

Elise smiled at Dylan. "It's his job."

"I can imagine. He came to my office this afternoon and claimed he intended to wait all night for me to return from my rounds at the hospital. He didn't have to, fortunately, since once my assistant called and told me there was a Dylan Colman waiting for me, I hurried back as soon as I could."

"Because I'd mentioned him to you," Elise surmised.

"Yes. We had a long talk, Dylan and I. He convinced me to follow him to Viento Blanco in my car, to come here and help you control your headaches so that you could get to the bottom of their cause."

"But that's what I wanted to tell you. I already know the cause," Elise said. "I *know*—"

Puzzled, she stopped at the expression in Dylan's eyes, still anguished. She realized he had said barely a word either, and she suddenly knew why. He had let her fight her battles herself, knew she must in order to be truly free of Keith. In order to be free to come to him, Dylan.

Yet there was another reason he hadn't spoken. She could see his doubts, and the very fear she'd vowed she'd face expanded in her chest. Was it too late for them both?

"Dr. Emerson, Aunt Char," Elise murmured, her gaze never leaving Dylan's. "Will you excuse us a minute? Oh, and Aunt Char, would you mind going over the rest of what happened with the doctor?"

"Certainly," Charlotte answered.

Side by side Elise and Dylan started down the cobbled street, their hands buried in the pockets of their raincoats. Twilight was falling, and the mist hovered in trance-inducing swirls, yet everything was bathed in a tangerine glow, as if sunlight hovered just out of reach.

She glanced at Dylan's profile in the murky light. It was pensive, sending another wave of apprehension through her.

"What are you thinking?" she asked.

That brought a half smile to his lips. "I'm thinking you've got a real spitfire of an aunt there."

"She's wonderful, isn't she?"

"Yes. And I'm thinking, so's her niece."

"I guess we're both pretty scrappy when it comes to holding on to those we love."

Dylan said nothing. But then, he already knew that she loved him.

They walked in silence for a few minutes.

"What are *you* thinking, Elise?" he asked, his voice subdued by the deadened air surrounding them.

"I was thinking how scary it is."

"What is?"

"How close I'd come to marrying that man. If you'd come back a few days later—"

"I should have come back months ago," Dylan interrupted with inwardly aimed impatience. "To think of you and him together..." His jaw clenched.

She put a hand on his sleeve. "But I'm not with Keith, Dylan. I'm with you. And the important thing is, you did come back in time."

"Did I?" he asked.

They stopped, and Elise saw that they stood near the same gap between two buildings where they'd first begun to put the pieces of their lives together. And she understood then. He didn't know that she remembered.

Dylan leaned a shoulder against the damp wall, facing her, his expression as inscrutable as it had been the last time they'd stood there. "Did I come back in time, Elise?" he asked again. "In time...for us?"

She reached out and brushed a damp shock of his ebony hair from his forehead. "You're thirty-two," she said. Her hand drifted over his cheek, down to his jaw. He closed his eyes, as if in pain, much as he had the first time she touched him this way. "And you got your striking bone structure from the Native American blood in you."

His eyes popped open. "How do you know that?"

"You told me, Dylan."

"I know, but..."

"I remember," she said softly. "Everything."

"I see." His gaze was impenetrable, though his shoulders tensed as if ready to receive a blow.

"I haven't been myself for so long," she went on, her voice low and musing. "Longer than since my accident, it seems. Almost since my parents died. It's been like part of me was gone, or slumbering somewhere, more than just my painting or health. It was as if I went into hibernation, wanted to be alone—so people couldn't hurt me anymore. But then I met you, and you pushed past all my defenses, showed me how I could love and be loved. And go on living. But even then I continued to have doubts that I could survive." Her voice dropped to a whisper. "That I even wanted to survive. It would have been so much easier not to."

"And now?" Dylan asked, his own voice husky with that incredible empathy she so loved in him. She lifted her eyes to his.

"Now I know that I came back for you, Dylan Colman. I have survived, through my own efforts. For myself, and for you and our love. And I found the piece of me that had been missing...*you.*"

She stepped closer and threaded her fingers through the hair at his temple, stroking the side of his head back to his nape as he had soothed his hand over her skull and given her relief through his touch. "I love you, Dylan. Now that I've found you again, I'm never, ever letting you go."

His arms slid around her, pulling her against him. "Just try it," he muttered as he seized her mouth with his. And through kisses—and tears—Elise told him how she remembered, what she remembered, why she remembered. He held her throughout, and the catharsis was complete.

He dried the wetness on her cheeks and lashes with his fingertips, then moistened them again with his lips. When his mouth came home to hers, she responded with every bit of her heart and soul, even as her body responded with the quickening of her pulse. For now she knew, in vivid detail, how much they had loved together, and though she was glad she had the memories, they were not enough.

She pressed closer and Dylan groaned with the increased contact. "God, I love you, Ellie," he said. "I don't think I'll ever get enough of you—"

His words were hushed against her lips, lost within her mouth. Then she felt a rumble of laughter start in his chest and vibrate upward. Elise pulled away and looked at him in curiosity. He was smiling, and it was the Dylan of her sketch who looked back at her.

"No, I'll never get enough of you," he said, "although we've certainly got the time now to try, don't we?"

Aunt Charlotte got her wedding after all. Elise and Dylan were married three days later, after a whirlwind of emergency preparations. Dr. Emerson ran Elise through a score of tests, gave her a complete physical and pronounced the young patient sound as a bell. Elise spent a few hours with Dr. Hathaway, the psychiatrist, who also deemed her well on her way to complete recovery. Dylan called in a few more favors and managed to expedite Elise's passport application and request for visa in record time. Most of his family was able to fly in, even on such short notice, and they all got to meet the woman Dylan had searched for and finally found.

Their wedding day dawned clear and sunny, a bit of fortuity that added to the specialness surrounding this couple. Elise refused to even consider wearing the muted pastel suit she'd intended for the civil ceremony she and Keith had planned. Instead, her tea-length dress was a luminescent white, contrasting brilliantly with Dylan's black tuxedo and dark good looks. They'd decided to have a church wedding, and as Elise walked up the aisle of Viento Blanco's tiny chapel toward the man who stood in the shaft of sunlight bathing the altar, she experienced a flash of déjà vu. It was as if she'd been there before, lived that moment before. But this wasn't a glimmer of latent memory. This was her future.

She knew, then, that she had found her destiny. And it was forever linked with this man.

Elise stepped forward into the sunlight as well, as Dylan handed her a single scarlet rose. "You needed something red," he murmured, "not borrowed or blue."

Sniffing the flower, she smiled at him. "You know red roses mean 'I love you.'"

"I do. But they also stand for courage, Ellie."

Tears filled her eyes. Yes, they'd both found each other.

Dylan caught her hand in his. They turned to face the minister and exchanged their vows, truly linking their lives, and completeness came home to nest in her.

The only sad note struck that day was after they'd exited the chapel and stood on its steps, when Charlotte came out for her hug of congratulation. Elise pressed her cheek against her aunt's and sniffed back tears as she realized she would soon bid this dear woman goodbye.

"I hate leaving you here by yourself," she said on a choked whisper.

"Now, child, don't you worry. I can take care of myself."

Elise pulled back and smiled through a blur. "You've certainly shown us all over the past few days that you can.

I'm glad, anyway, that Dr. Emerson recommended her accountant to take care of your affairs and volunteered to keep in touch with you herself." She shot a grateful smile at her doctor, who stood nearby with Dylan. "And Dylan and I will be back in a few months. We're hoping he'll be able to work from D.C., without having to go overseas so much. And once we've saved some money, we're going to buy a cabin in Oregon. Perhaps we'll be able to persuade you to move close to us."

"I appreciate the thought, dear, but Viento Blanco is my home. I'll miss you, but I can see how happy you are. And that's all that matters."

"I'll come back to visit," Elise murmured around the lump in her throat.

"I'll be here," Aunt Charlotte said.

"Yes," she rested her palm against the soft paper-thin skin of her aunt's cheek, "you've always been here for me."

"Look!" someone cried.

Everyone turned. In the distance a cloud approached, stark white against the bright blue of the sky. The people watched as the billow rose and fell, undulating like a wave on the ocean. As it drew closer, they realized what it was: thousands of pearl white butterflies. The multitude swooped toward them, riding the southerly wind, and circled the church's spire, swirling like a silvery dust devil.

And then it was snowing butterflies. The movement of their wings created the subtlest of breezes. They covered the trees and bushes, the heads and shoulders of the people who gazed around them in delight.

"I'd heard of this happening when I was a little girl, but I've never seen it in my seventy years in Viento Blanco!" Charlotte exclaimed.

"So *this* is the 'white wind,'" Dylan said as he tucked his bride snug against his side. Butterflies rained down on his black hair and tuxedoed shoulders. He held out an open hand and one even landed on his palm.

"I don't know," Charlotte answered. "But I do know we don't get migrations of any sort coming through here unless the conditions are just right. It takes perfect weather on the precise day the butterflies are passing by. They're drawn by the sun and warm breeze off the ocean, you see.'' She extended her arms, and a row of butterflies lit on her like pins on a clothesline. ''It must be a hundred years since this happened last! What a happy coincidence on this day of days!'' she cried.

''No coincidence,'' Dylan whispered into Elise's ear. ''It's fate.''

She turned her head and brushed her mouth against his. Fate or destiny... faith or hope. Or simply a reason to believe. Any and all of these had brought her back to life—a life with this man. And she was thankful that both she and the missionaries had known what they were doing.

A month later, Charlotte received a flat package stamped with all sorts of foreign postmarks. She opened it quickly and discovered a small painting of a landscape. It was of Viento Blanco as it had been on the day of Elise and Dylan's wedding, from a bird's-eye view—''or a butterfly's-eye view,'' Charlotte thought on a whimsical note—as if the artist had hovered above the scene below. The butterflies, their formation looking exactly like a sail full of wind, stood out against the vivid blue of the sky and the deep green hills surrounding the town. The painting was signed in the lower right-hand corner: *E. Colman*.

That dear child, Charlotte thought fondly as she hung the painting on her bedroom wall. ''She didn't have to do this so soon after her marriage,'' the old woman *tsk*ed even as she stood back and admired the landscape. ''There certainly wasn't any rush. She had time. All the time in the world.''

* * * * *

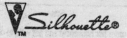

Take 4 bestselling love stories FREE

Plus get a FREE surprise gift!

Special Limited-time Offer

Mail to Silhouette Reader Service™

3010 Walden Avenue
P.O. Box 1867
Buffalo, N.Y. 14269-1867

YES! Please send me 4 free Silhouette Romance™ novels and my free surprise gift. Then send me 6 brand-new novels every month, which I will receive months before they appear in bookstores. Bill me at the low price of $2.19 each plus 25¢ delivery and applicable sales tax, if any.* That's the complete price and—compared to the cover prices of $2.75 each—quite a bargain! I understand that accepting the books and gift places me under no obligation ever to buy any books. I can always return a shipment and cancel at any time. Even if I never buy another book from Silhouette, the 4 free books and the surprise gift are mine to keep forever.

215 BPA ANRP

Name	(PLEASE PRINT)
Address	Apt. No.
City	State Zip

This offer is limited to one order per household and not valid to present Silhouette Romance™ subscribers. *Terms and prices are subject to change without notice. Sales tax applicable in N.Y.

USROM-04R   ©1990 Harlequin Enterprises Limited

MONTANA MAVERICKS™

Stories that capture living and loving beneath the Big Sky, where legends live on...and the mystery is just beginning.

Watch for the sizzling debut of
MONTANA MAVERICKS in August with

ROGUE STALLION

by Diana Palmer

A powerful tale of simmering desire and mystery!

And don't miss a minute of the loving as the mystery continues with:

THE WIDOW AND THE RODEO MAN
by Jackie Merritt (September)
SLEEPING WITH THE ENEMY
by Myrna Temte (October)
THE ONCE AND FUTURE WIFE
by Laurie Paige (November)
THE RANCHER TAKES A WIFE
by Jackie Merritt (December)
and many more of your favorite authors!

Only from V Silhouette®

where passion lives.

MAV1

Silhouette

SPECIAL EDITION

TM

That
SPECIAL
Woman!

50th book

BABY BLESSED
Debbie Macomber

Molly Larabee didn't expect her reunion with
estranged husband Jordan to be quite so explosive.
Their tumultuous past was filled with memories of
tragedy—and love. Rekindling familiar passions left
Molly with an unexpected blessing...and suddenly a
future with Jordan was again worth fighting for!

Don't miss Debbie Macomber's fiftieth book,
BABY BLESSED, available in July!

She's friend, wife, mother—she's you! And beside
each **Special Woman** stands a wonderfully
special man. It's a celebration of our heroines—
and the men who become part of their lives.

TSW794

WHERE THE HEART IS

Get set for an exciting new series from
bestselling author

ELIZABETH AUGUST

Join us for the first book:

THE FORGOTTEN HUSBAND

Amnesia kept Eloise from knowing the real reason she'd
married cold, distant Jonah Tavish. But brief moments of sweet
passion kept her searching for the truth. Can anyone help Eloise
and Jonah rediscover love?

Meet Sarah Orman in *WHERE THE HEART IS*. She has a way
of showing up just when people need her most. And with her
wit and down-to-earth charm, she brings couples together—
for keeps.

Available in July, only from

Silhouette
R O M A N C E™

BABY'S CHOICE

Those mischievous matchmaking babies are back, as
Marie Ferrarella's Baby's Choice series continues in
August with MOTHER ON THE WING (SR #1026).

Frank Harrigan could hardly explain his sudden desire
to fly to Seattle. Sure, an old friend had written to him
out of the blue, but there was something else.... Then he
spotted Donna McCollough, or rather, she fell right into his lap.
And from that moment on, they were powerless to interfere
with what angelic fate had lovingly ordained.

Continue to share in the wonder of life and love, as
babies-in-waiting handpick the most perfect parents,
only in

Silhouette
R O M A N C E™

It's our 1000th Silhouette Romance™, and we're celebrating!

And to say "THANK YOU" to our wonderful readers, we would like to send you a

FREE AUSTRIAN CRYSTAL BRACELET

This special bracelet truly captures the spirit of CELEBRATION 1000! and is a stunning complement to any outfit! And it can be yours FREE just for enjoying SILHOUETTE ROMANCE™.

FREE GIFT OFFER

To receive your free gift, complete the certificate according to directions. Be certain to enclose the required number of proofs-of-purchase. Requests must be received no later than August 31, 1994. Please allow 6 to 8 weeks for receipt of order. Offer good while quantities of gifts last. Offer good in U.S. and Canada only.

And that's not all! Readers can also enter our...

CELEBRATION 1000! SWEEPSTAKES

In honor of our 1000th SILHOUETTE ROMANCE™, we'd like to award $1000 to a lucky reader!

As an added value every time you send in a completed offer certificate with the correct amount of proofs-of-purchase, your name will automatically be entered in our CELEBRATION 1000! Sweepstakes. The sweepstakes features a grand prize of $1000. PLUS, 1000 runner-up prizes of a FREE SILHOUETTE ROMANCE™, autographed by one of CELEBRATION 1000!'s special featured authors will be awarded. These volumes are sure to be cherished for years to come, a true commemorative keepsake.

DON'T MISS YOUR OPPORTUNITY TO WIN! ENTER NOW!

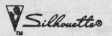

CELOFFER

CELEBRATION 1000! FREE GIFT OFFER

ORDER INFORMATION:

To receive your free AUSTRIAN CRYSTAL BRACELET, send three original proof-of-purchase coupons from any SILHOUETTE ROMANCE™ title published in April through July 1994 with the Free Gift Certificate completed, plus $1.75 for postage and handling (check or money order—please do not send cash) payable to Silhouette Books CELEBRATION 1000! Offer. Hurry! Quantities are limited.

FREE GIFT CERTIFICATE   096 KBM

Name:_____

Address:_____

City:_____ State/Prov.:_____ Zip/Postal:_____

Mail this certificate, three proofs-of-purchase and check or money order to CELEBRATION 1000! Offer, Silhouette Books, 3010 Walden Avenue, P.O. Box 9057, Buffalo, NY 14269-9057 or P.O. Box 622, Fort Erie, Ontario L2A 5X3. Please allow 4-6 weeks for delivery. Offer expires August 31, 1994.

PLUS

Every time you submit a completed certificate with the correct number of proofs-of-purchase, you are automatically entered in our CELEBRATION 1000! SWEEPSTAKES to win the GRAND PRIZE of $1000 CASH! PLUS, 1000 runner-up prizes of a FREE Silhouette Romance™, autographed by one of CELEBRATION 1000!'s special featured authors, will be awarded. No purchase or obligation necessary to enter. See below for alternate means of entry and how to obtain complete sweepstakes rules.

CELEBRATION 1000! SWEEPSTAKES
NO PURCHASE OR OBLIGATION NECESSARY TO ENTER

You may enter the sweepstakes without taking advantage of the CELEBRATION 1000! FREE GIFT OFFER by hand-printing on a 3" x 5" card (mechanical reproductions are not acceptable) your name and address and mailing it to: CELEBRATION 1000! Sweepstakes, P.O. Box 9057, Buffalo, NY 14269-9057 or P.O. Box 622, Fort Erie, Ontario L2A 5X3. Limit: one entry per envelope. Entries must be sent via First Class mail and be received no later than August 31, 1994. No liability is assumed for lost, late or misdirected mail.

Sweepstakes is open to residents of the U.S. (except Puerto Rico) and Canada, 18 years of age or older. All federal, state, provincial, municipal and local laws apply. Offer void wherever prohibited by law. Odds of winning dependent on the number of entries received. For complete rules, send a self-addressed, stamped envelope to: CELEBRATION 1000! Rules, P.O. Box 4200, Blair, NE 68009.

 ONE PROOF OF PURCHASE

096KBM